A LITTLE LOWER THAN THE ANGELS

A
LITTLE LOWER
THAN
THE ANGELS

Geraldine McCaughrean

Oxford University Press
Oxford Toronto Melbourne

Oxford University Press, Walton Street,
Oxford OX2 6DP

Oxford New York Toronto
Delhi Bombay Calcutta Madras Karachi
Petaling Jaya Singapore Hong Kong Tokyo
Nairobi Dar es Salaam Cape Town
Melbourne Auckland

and associated companies in
Berlin Ibadan

Oxford is a trade mark of Oxford University Press

British Library Cataloguing in Publication Data

McCaughrean, Geraldine
A little lower than the angels.
I. Title
823'.914[J]   PZ7
ISBN 0–19–271561–5

Typeset by Fontwise
Printed in Great Britain by
Biddles Ltd, Guildford

For
JOHN and the ANGEL

'What is man, that thou art mindful of him?
And the son of man, that thou visiteth him?
For thou hast made him a little lower than the angels,
and hast crowned him with glory and honour.'

Psalm 8:4–5

CHAPTER ONE

TOO MUCH BLOOD IN THE BRAIN

ONE MOMENT he was holding them—the mallet in one hand, the spike in the other—and the next he was upside down, hanging by one foot from the rope. The loop closed round his ankle: he could feel the hemp biting into his skin. His knee, thigh and pelvis seemed on the point of parting company. He was swinging, suspended, his arms flailing and his hair hanging away from his skull. Blood hammered inside his head.

The Mason, who had been standing underneath, bent down and picked up the mallet and the spike and weighed them in his hands. The sun shining through the stained glass on to his pock-marked face turned it a terrifying green and red. 'You mindless little toad. You half-wit yard of kennel-water. You could have done for me, dropping them!' He made as if to throw the tools back up at the boy, but did not let go of them. There was nothing Gabriel could do to protect himself, strung up by one foot and just within the Mason's reach. He took hold of Gabriel's hair and set him swinging, so that the boy crashed against the wall. 'Look at you. What good are you, anyway? Look at your pretty yellow curls. If I'd wanted an apprentice with curls I'd have signed on a girl. Next time do me a favour—break your neck. Get him down, Squit.'

The second apprentice, Squit, squatting on the church floor with his head between his big, dirty knees, squinted up at Gabriel and thumbed his nose,

1

babbling, 'Girl! Girl! Girls got curls!'

Suddenly, hanging there from the roof of the church by one foot, waiting for that idiot Squit to slacken the rope and let him down, everything became horribly clear to Gabriel. It was like looking back on the route of a dreadful, uphill journey, from the last summit.

The Mason did not want an apprentice stonemason. He had never been interested in teaching his craft. Small boys irritated him. He could hardly stomach them near him. All the Mason wanted was the fee from Gabriel's parents, the twenty shillings they had paid to put the boy in the Mason's charge and have him taught a trade.

Now there was a second apprentice—Squit—and talk of a third. But the Mason did not teach. They learned anything they learned by watching him. They were given the arduous jobs—squaring off corners, rubbing down chisel marks, darkening down the Mason's accidental chips. And they saw precious little of the twenty shillings spent on food or clothing for either of them. It was true: if Gabriel had fallen and killed himself, he *would* have done the Mason a favour—made room for another apprentice, another twenty unearned shillings. Perhaps that was why he was hauled up to work with one foot in a loop of rope, instead of a basket like the Mason or fat Squit. Perhaps the Mason *wanted* him to have a fatal accident . . .

The thought made Gabriel want to shout out, 'Help! Don't let me die!' He wanted his parents. He wanted to break his apprentice's bond and go home. He hated himself for wanting it. Most of all, he hated himself for wanting to cry. He was glad that the blood turning him blue in the face and pounding in his eyeballs kept back the tears.

Squit loosed off the rope and let him fall hard to the floor head-first. It was too much for Gabriel. He pressed the heels of his hands into his eye-sockets, squatted back on his heels and sobbed. He was, after all, only eleven.

'If my father knew . . .' he began to say, meaning to share his flash of insight with Squit. But when he opened his eyes and took his hands away, Squit was far away, dancing round the nave singing, 'Girls! Girls! Girls got curls!' And pushed close up against Gabriel's face was the Mason's pock-marked grin. 'Knew? Knew what? That he's fathered a grizzling girl? 'Spect he's glad to be rid of you. I did him a favour. I got you away from that coddling mother of yours—always washing you—always slicking you like a cat. And we moved on, didn't we? We be'nt going back, are we? You're bonded to me now, sure as a brand on a cow. You're mine, you smear of lard. Mine to spit on. Got it?' As his caked, yellow eyes travelled over Gabriel's face and head, what he saw caused him such disgust that his sweat-wet cheeks distorted as if they were melting. He searched for the worst insult in his huge mental library of insults and mouthed it into Gabriel's face through bared fangs. '*Pretty boy!*'

As Gabriel put his foot back into the rope loop and was hauled back up jerkingly into the church roof, he felt too weary to hate the Mason. It took all the strength he could muster to despise himself—his pretty face, his curly hair, his cowardly tears. It was probably true: his father was probably glad to see the back of him. 'Couldn't go home anyway. Don't know the way back,' he thought. He looked down at the church—at the green and red sunbeams falling on the Mason's scabby hair, and he thought, 'How ridiculous. To think he would only take us for the bond-money. Ridiculous. Too much blood in the brain, I suppose.'

The Mason brooded on the events of the day. Every

time Gabriel looked round, he found the Mason's eyes on him. It made him nervous and clumsy.

Out of doors, excited people kept streaming past the church. Something out of the ordinary was happening. The Mason and his boys had to leave the church while a Mass took place. 'Feast day for some local saint,' he muttered, still eyeing Gabriel up and down contemptuously. Gabriel gathered that it was not so much the saint who was local as one of his bones, which rested in the church treasure chest and which once a year was taken out and venerated. The whole town took part—a holiday all of their own.

Squatting around in the muddy porch, wondering whether *he* was at the Mass or not, Gabriel watched the Mason eating bread and chives. He watched the Sacristan corner a stray dog in the side-chapel and throw it out of doors. He listened to the men gossiping near the door: on their knees or standing, they did not let the service interrupt their conversation.

'Well? Are you going?' said one.

'It's not Guild. It's not local men. Just a pack of gypsies. Not as good as locals,' said the other.

'Do it all year. Must be better. Stands to reason.'

'Do it all year? What kind of work's that? It's unholy, I call it.'

'Got the church steps, didn't they? Church must favour them.'

'Groat-and-farthing show,' said his friend suspiciously.

The first man left a moment's silence then said temptingly, 'You wouldn't believe Hell! I seen it on the road coming. Never seen a Hell like it!'

'Might stay, then. Might,' said his friend grudgingly.

'Did you hear that?' Gabriel whispered to Squit. '"Never seen a Hell like it." What's that mean?'

Squit had not been listening.

They stared at the clothes of the miller and his wife who were first out of the church. 'That's velvet,' said Gabriel, chafing his shoulderblades against the porch bench because his own hessian jacket itched.

'You'd like a frock made out of that, would you?' the Mason hissed in his ear. 'A pretty blue frock to match your eyes?' Gabriel bit his lip and put his hands over his ears and did not speak again.

Directly in front of the church was an area of brick paving. In wet weather the merchants and their wives, arriving by wagon, did not need to muddy their Sunday shoes. The roots of the yew trees were lifting the bricks here and there, and all the cracks bulged with grass and weeds and little flowers.

As Gabriel sat in the church porch, a couple of young men came rushing round the church and began erecting a trellis at either side of the terrace, and draping the trellises in cloth. It was like putting blinkers on the church. A great commotion broke out as two huge carts arrived. A wagon larger than any Gabriel had seen before was struggling through the churchyard gate ahead of another, smaller cart, loaded with barrels, ladders, coils of rope and trestles. The large one had once been painted gold—patches of gilt still clung to it here and there like moulting velvet on a deer's antlers. It was open on one side, and along the edge sat four or five people, their legs dangling only about as far as the hubs of the huge wheels, so high were the axles. A weather-vane in the shape of an iron dog speckled with rust and gilt wagged at the top of a cane pole at one corner, with ribbon streamers blowing from its neck. A banner above the tailgate had flapped itself to tatters and been mended many times, though its colours were faded by sun and rain and its pattern was indecipherable. But on the inside panels of the three cart-sides, brightly painted flowers and animals, stooks of corn and grapevines as well as a rainbow looked freshly painted. Heaps of cloth and clothes stirred in the base of the cart as the wind made them billow.

The second, sideless, flat-backed cart sagged suddenly as one wheel dropped into a newly filled grave, and several of the barrels were spilled and rolled away with a hollow cacophony, banging against each other.

The Mass was over, but the townspeople did not disperse out of the churchyard. They stood about watching the carts roll into place on the brick terrace. Some burly women who had carried stools to Mass, set them down again facing the church door and the carts, and settled themselves, hands folded in their laps, as if prepared for a long wait. They looked like broody chickens sitting on their eggs.

The empty barrels were used to support a huge trestle table alongside the two carts. The stage was ready.

'Did you never see a play?' said Squit, full of scorn.

'We live nine miles from a town,' said Gabriel, feeling his neck go red. 'I never went but twice.' He added defensively, 'I've seen a fair ... What is it, anyway?'

'Well, it's a play, isn't it,' said Squit, shrugging in the way that meant he was hoping not to be asked for more details.

'You mean it's a game?'

'No, a *play*, stupid. People pretending to be other people—Noah and Jesus and God and snakes and things.'

Gabriel looked sideways at Squit and wondered what nonsense he was talking now.

'Don't you worry your head about it, pretty boy,' said the Mason with a threatening, soft-spoken spite. '*You* won't be seeing it, will you?' And he picked up the boys by their hessian, and pushed them back into the church.

As Gabriel began work again, up in the roof, and his eyelids and nose and hair and ears got clogged with the dark-grey stone dust, he could hear the crowd settle facing the stage. He could hear the murmured excitement, the shrill bleat of women laughing. Then the church door banged open, and a voice shouted in: 'We can't have you banging on in here . . . we can hear you the other side of town. Come and watch the Mystery, why don't you?'

The Mason seethed. He looked at one apprentice, then the other. Their eager, hopeful faces seemed to sting him like wasps. 'There's work needs doing,' he snarled at the figure in the doorway.

'Look at it my way,' said the man in the doorway patiently. 'You can come and watch, or you can carry on banging and I'll take your chisel and your lads' chisels and I'll push them down your uncivil throat. Today I'm God, and what God says is, and always will be—evermore—Amen. Got it?'

And that was how Gabriel came to see his first play.

A row of women who were sharing a bench waved to him and shuffled sideways, making room. He squeezed in between them, embarrassed at the touch of their plump, creamy arms. They smelt of fresh bread and lavender.

''Course, they're not *our* men,' one confided in his ear. 'They're not locals. Did you ever hear of such a thing? Worthless outsiders, I dare say. But just look at Heaven. Isn't that a thing?'

He followed the direction of her eyes and saw . . . *Heaven*. He had walked past it on the way out of the church without even seeing it. At the top of a flowery hill, on a cloud as large as a toboggan, sat a smiling, sunburned figure in a glittering robe, and reclining at his feet along another ridge of cloud, lay a fat, sleepy angel, his skirts billowing in the wind.

But Gabriel could not keep his eyes on Heaven, much as he wanted to. He tried not to look to the left-hand side of the stage, where a hideous head gaped, its fanged jaws wide enough to swallow a grown man. Its tongue lolled on to the stage, and smoke trickled gently but continuously out of the back of its throat. As he stared in horrid fascination, and the hair stirred on the back of his neck, the creature's eye cracked open, blazing green, and looking directly at him.

The women along the bench squealed and accidently squashed Gabriel between them as they breathed in. He did not notice: he thought it was fright that had stopped him breathing. He could not understand why, a moment later, there was cheery laughter and a round of applause.

'Bless you, child, it's only a play,' said a woman whose arm he had grabbed, pressing his dirty face into her dress. 'That's the Mouth of Hell that is, where all the damned souls go on the Day of Judgement for being wicked. Gobble, gobble! Ha-ha-ha!'

Out on to the slopes of Heaven stepped a tall dark-haired boy. He put a recorder to his lips and began to play. And from somewhere beneath his feet, an invisible fountain of music burst into the startled sky. So magical was the sound that a tree raised itself up off the wooden platform. A big red apple swung from it like a shop sign. Some of the audience began to sing, but their singing petered out as a gruesome man/lizard slithered out of the gaping, smoking Mouth of Hell. His horned, scaly, hooded face peered out into the audience and grinned. He was booed loudly, and the woman alongside Gabriel took an apple core out of her skirt pocket and threw it. It hit the church door.

> 'Out, out, unhappy me
> Who lately thought to be
> The proudest of them all
> —Thrown down from Heaven to Hell!
> Once was I angel-bright
> The fairest golden-winged sight
> That ever you did see,
> But now, unhappy me!'

Gabriel opened his eyes and ears as wide as windows, and in flew sights and sounds such as he had never known—a man and a woman in red and white cloaks, animals and angels singing, and God Himself perched cross-legged upon the slopes of Heaven. When it came to an end, he could not tell what he had seen and what he had imagined. When the Devil described the fiery regions of Hell, it was both wonderful and terrible. He wept for the poor bare lady and gentleman, Adam and Eve, thrown out of the lovely Garden of Eden because they ate the big red apple. He knew what they were feeling. He had felt just the same, as the Mason's cart pulled away from his own little cottage and he looked back and saw his mother waving and waving and waving . . .

The woman on the bench thrust her apron into Gabriel's face and wiped his nose. 'Don't take on so, child. It's only a play. I told you.'

The play was over. The Devil had crawled, on his belly, back into the Mouth of Hell, with a lump of charcoal in his mouth. And the fat, billowing angel had gone back up to Heaven to sit beside God. The clouds had hidden them both from sight. Gabriel knew the story: he could not remember why, but he had always known the story. How many times in this first year of his apprenticeship had he seen stained-glass windows showing the selfsame story? But to see it happen—then and there—in front of his eyes! That was different!

'It's the most wonderful thing I've ever seen,' he whispered in the woman's ear, and she wiped his nose again with her hand.

'Bless him, but he's a good-looking little lad, isn't he?' she said to her friends along the bench. 'All those lovely golden curls. I wish I had hair as pretty. Who's he you're with? Your father? Thought not. There's none of his ugly mug in you.'

'Is that a fact?' It was the Mason's voice. One hand

9

took hold of Gabriel's long hair and pulled him up on tip-toe. The other, taking hold of his jerkin, lifted him backwards clear over the bench, so that his feet knocked against a fat woman's head and sent her headclothes tumbling. 'Big bully,' said the women, but they did not come to Gabriel's help.

The Mason carried him, rigid with fright, off the brick terrace, round the side of the church, and behind the big old yew trees. Squit was nowhere to be seen.

'Hairy little monkey. A sheep's got less hair than you. You're a flea-catcher, that's what you are. How many fleas have you got in that ticking you call hair?' The abuse poured down on Gabriel as though he had stood under an open window and a bucket of refuse had been tipped out on his head. 'Well, I've got a mattress needs stuffing. And that hair of yours will do instead of feathers.' The Mason threw Gabriel to the ground, without letting go of his hair, and drew a knife out of his belt.

'No! Not my hair! Not my hair!' Gabriel put his hands over his head and pulled away with all his might. 'My mother told me . . . I promised my mother!'

How could he explain? How could he tell, in the space of a single breath, the story his mother had spent so long in telling—about Samson the Strong Man whose strength was all in his hair. 'Samson!' he screamed. 'In the Bible!'

The Mason knocked him face-down to the ground and sat on his legs. 'Samson?' He roared a vicious, tormenting laugh. 'Did she tell you you were a second Samson? Well then, I'm Delilah!'

No, Gabriel was not a strong man, even with his hair. But what would he be without it? The knife dragged once through his curls with a rasping noise, and already he felt his legs powerless to move where the Mason sat on them. Would he be paralysed? Limp, like a dead chicken? Already he could not feel his feet. He opened his mouth to scream but all that came out

10

was a reedy croak. Already his voice was weak. 'Not my hair! *Please not my hair!*'

Suddenly the yew trees gave a convulsive shiver and someone from the audience, strolling away from the play, poked his head through the low branches. He saw the Mason pulling back Gabriel's head and he saw the knife. 'Hey! Murder! There's a knave here cutting a lad's throat!'

'No!' said the Mason and sprang to his feet.

That was the last Gabriel heard. He dug his toes into the soft soil and sprinted away down the side of the church.

It was like his nightmares when demons were chasing him, and his feet were wading through tar. He blamed his cut hair for the slowness of his legs. At the corner of the church he took the skin off one palm, swinging round the end buttress.

All the way round the church he ran, and out on to the brick terrace again. Then, taking his eyes off the ground, he saw his way barred by crowds of people. The audience had hardly dispersed at all, though their backs were turned now. The words kept whispering in his ears (or was too much blood pounding in them?) 'Broken bond! Broken bond! Broken bond!'

Every moment he expected the Mason to grab him from behind, wielding his knife. He ran at the church wall, leapt up at it, failed to get a grip and fell back on to a grave. He turned back towards the church steps, thinking to take refuge in the dark building. Perhaps he could even plead sanctuary and live in the church for the rest of his life, safe from the punishment of the law, begging bread from the worshippers. He would starve! Who would help a boy who broke his apprentice's bond?

All these thoughts—so many unbearable thoughts— were swept through his head by the river of pounding blood. He found his route to the church door barred by the stage—the cart and the trestle platform and the

Hill of Heaven and the monstrous, gaping Mouth of Hell!

Here was the space where he had seen such things as he had thought only the saints in Heaven witnessed. Such holy, biblical things! Part of him knew that they were only men dressed up and pretending. And yet while he had watched, he had been there—there, in the Garden of Eden. Surely it was a magic space, up above the cart wheels, out of time, out of place—a holy space that would swallow up a running boy and dissolve him from sight.

One foot on the spoke of the cart wheel, over the rim of the stage, and Gabriel sprang on to the platform. It seemed a bare, splintery waste all of a sudden, not a garden at all. He looked up to the Hill of Heaven, but God was no longer perched there! And how could a boy who had broken his bond dare to set foot in Heaven anyway? Hell was the place for such a boy, such a girlish, loathsome, curl-haired, wicked, unforgivable boy.

The Mouth of Hell gaped at him; the mechanical eye stared at him; the throat gargled smoke. Beyond the gullet he could just see the Devil—what?—writhing in sulphurous torment?

On the far side of the church, the Mason strode into sight pulling along, like a great dray-horse, two unhappy looking youths. 'I tell you, I was giving the runt a haircut, that's all! He's my apprentice! His parents pay me good money to look after him . . . All that hair . . . it's not healthy. It's spoiling his eyesight. Only today he fell out of the roof . . .' The youths let go, embarrassed, apologizing to the Mason.

Gabriel made the sign of the cross and jumped into the Mouth of Hell. The smell of burning pricked the back of his nose. He wriggled into the red gullet of Hell. Two hands from beyond reached into his armpits and pulled him through.

It was God.

CHAPTER TWO

THE ANGEL GABRIEL

'GET DOWN in the barrel, son. Get right in and keep
your head down.'

Gabriel had no breath to argue. One of the barrels
supporting the trestle stage was pushed only half-way
under. Gabriel was able to slide into it, head-first,
over the edge of the platform, and lay curled up in the
bottom, as still as a hedgehog in hibernation.

After a year or a month or possibly half an hour,
God's face looked in. 'What are you then? A
cutpurse?'

'No!' Gabriel's voice came back at him off the sides
of the barrel. 'He was going to cut my hair! I
promised my mother! She said never to cut my hair!'

The face looked none the wiser, and shoulders
shrugged into view. 'Your mother's not stupid. It's
fine hair. I could do something with that hair.'

'He said he'd stuff a mattress with it!' whispered
Gabriel hoarsely. The fumes from the beer that had
once been stored in the barrel were making him feel
rather sick. When he climbed out, his legs were red
behind the knees and as wobbly as two pieces of
string.

'Who? That big oaf of a stonemason? The one who
wanted to go on banging through my play? You're his
apprentice?'

What was the point of lying? God probably knew

everything. 'I ran away. I've broken my bond. Must I go back? Must I do penance?'

God did not seem to be listening. He was tugging at his lower lip and walking slowly round Gabriel. 'What do you think of this, Lucie?'

The Devil, wriggling out of the last of his knitted tail, wiped the shiny grease off his face and neck before strolling over. He said, 'Liked our play, didn't you boy? I saw you over there, with the tears running down.'

Gabriel was galled with shame, though of course he could have expected the Devil to betray him. Guiltily he wiped away the girlish tear-stains with the back of his hand.

'What's the matter? What's wrong with a few tears? The badge of a civilized man,' said the Devil, and wandered off in his short breeches, his ribs showing even through the dark curly hair on his back. He had thin ankles, too, and moved for all the world like a wolf.

'What's your name?' said God.

'Gabriel, sir.'

'Like the angel, eh? The Archangel Gabriel. Like name, like nature, so they say. Like face, like fortune . . . I could use you, son.' As he spoke, and then sneezed, his head was surrounded by a halo of white, just like a saint in a stained-glass window. Flour was emanating from his hair. It was an awesome sight. 'How would you like to join us for a while? Food and kinship. A job your dear mother would be proud to see you in. No more beatings than you deserve. And safe out of this town before your master takes it too hard.'

Gabriel's jaw dropped. 'But I'm no good! I only do corners and finishing!'

God seemed momentarily perplexed. 'You only do corners and finishing?'

'And cleaning up. And anyway, I don't have any tools!'

14

A fresh cloud of flour came sprinkling down as God burst out laughing. The more his hair lost its white, the younger God was growing. 'But I don't want you for a stonechipper! I want you for an angel! Keep your shirt clean. That's all you have to do. Keep your shirt clean and your mouth shut. I won't get you to speak yet awhile. Lucie's got a daughter. She can do something with you—clean you up. Whatever else you do, *don't thieve.*'

It was a strange commandment. Gabriel had never in his life contemplated stealing so much as a flea from a dog. His mother and father had raised him to be a law-abiding Christian. But he did not mind God saying it, especially when he felt the kindly grip on his shoulder. It felt good.

The Devil had put on his clothes—dark, close-fitting clothes—and had come sloping back. Always placing one foot directly in front of the other gave him a slinking walk. He was told to put Gabriel in the charge of his daughter, and led the way. *He* did not put a hand on Gabriel's shoulder. 'I'm Lucie,' he said gruffly, 'because I always play Lucifer the Devil. He's Garvey, but you'd best call him Master. He'd prefer it. What he said about thieving—it's important. We need to be liked. We need to be respectable. One grain of trouble would gall the clergy and the councillors like a pin under a saddle. We're pioneers, boy, breaking new ground—planting new footprints on God's old Earth. There's none like us. Instead of plays being acted by the city craftsmen once a year, we've made a craft of play-acting. It's our profession. We don't do it once a year—we do it all year round— wherever the town councillors or the Abbot will pay us to put on a show.'

'I never saw a play before,' said Gabriel, to indicate in the politest possible way that he did not understand one word of what Lucie was telling him.

'Is that a fact? Is that a fact?' Lucie turned and

looked at him with piercing black eyes. 'You liked it, though?'

'I think it's the most wonderful thing I ever saw.'

Lucie considered this and nodded his head. 'Shame to spoil it for you, then,' he said tartly, and walked off, leaving Gabriel face to face with the recorder-player he had seen on stage. It wasn't a boy at all. It was Lucifer's daughter.

Izzie had the same pinched, dark features as her father and the same lank black hair but cut shorter. She walked round Gabriel with the same wolfish lope, then said, 'Hide in the wagon until we're out of town. You could get us all into trouble.'

Hell was a wooden arch with a cloth tunnel behind it and a simple catch holding shut the green eye. It smoked because there was a length of tarry rope nailed up behind the gullet which Lucie set alight before going on stage. God reached Heaven by climbing a ladder behind the wooden scenery. His world was peopled by half a dozen ragged individuals who had followed an assortment of callings, from seasonal shearing to thatching, cowherding to churchyard sexton. Mischief or discontent, a hard master or some family tragedy that made home hateful to them had shuffled together these jacks and knaves. All they had in common—Hob and Jack, Lucie and Garvey, John and Simon, Adam of Wendle, and the youth who played Eve—was a knowledge of the words of the Mysteries, some or all. Their affection for the plays varied. Some were there because, well, elsewhere they would starve. Some would have starved rather than give up the playing. The music was played by two musicians, Rolande and Ydrys, sitting cross-legged under the cart with a hurdy-gurdy, a reed-pipe, a drum and a shawm, all hidden from sight by a straw bale. On a windy day, guy ropes were needed to hold the flat scenery upright.

Gabriel quickly discovered why a replacement was needed for the angel. They left behind the pot-bellied shearer who had played him previously. They left him slumped in a drunken stupor against the church wall. Lucie forced a penny into his soft, sleeping palm, dumped his shearing tools in his lap, and pulled his cap down over his face in the hope that nobody would recognize him for one of the players.

In the next town the Abbot politely told them they were not wanted. The craftsmen of the local Guilds had been performing a play on the Feast of Corpus Christi for eighty years. No outsiders could do it better, and the city's working men and women were too busy to waste another day in idleness.

'In the west, the Guildsmen threw stones,' said Izzie. 'When once we've been to a place, we're liked. You liked us.'

She had a bald, stark way of speaking, never looking Gabriel in the eye but staring over his shoulder with a slight frown creasing her curd-yellow forehead. Before Gabriel acted for the first time, she spent hours brushing his hair and fluffing it out with a hazel twig into a frizzy golden cloud, quite indifferent to his squeaks and ouches. It was as if she were arranging flowers or carding wool. It was just one of her many tasks.

She made his costume, cutting down a white linen shirt and fitting it tight up round the neck. Nobody asked her to make it. She made all the costumes. It was one of her jobs. Her father left things with her for mending, like a sheep leaves its wool on a fence, in passing. She always had some piece of sewing stuck in her belt while she cooked. (Preparing meals for the players was another of her jobs.) She washed down the horses if they started to look or smell disreputable.

So she washed down Gabriel on the day he first played an angel.

The ladder trembled as soon as he put one bare foot on it. He stood there, one foot up, one foot down, and watched the top of the ladder bounce against the rickety scenery. He was mesmerized.

'Is that ladder nervous again?' said a quiet voice behind him. 'You'd think it would have stopped shaking by now. But no. Every time a new player sets foot on it, it starts to shake. Pay it no heed.' And a green-gloved hand reached over his shoulder to hold the ladder firm. Gabriel turned and looked straight into Lucie's green-stained face glistening with grease; a leather forked tongue was clenched between his teeth, and his black hair was slicked down with water in front of the green knitted hood. Gabriel went up the ladder two rungs at a time, and stood sweating behind his cloud. All he could hear was his heart beating. Perhaps the audience had picked up their stools and gone home. He was not sorry.

After Izzie finished playing her recorder, it was her job to loosen off the ropes and allow the scenery clouds to flop forwards on their hinges, revealing God and all His angels . . . God and His angel. The cloud in front of Gabriel flopped down. He bent his knees, hoping to stay hidden.

'Aaaah!' A long, sentimental gust of female sighs burst from the audience. They were all faces—just a mass of white ovals, like a dish of eggs. Viewed from so high up, their bodies were foreshortened and hidden by the faces in front. They looked so eager, so willing to be pleased. Gabriel put his flat trumpet to his lips and pretended to blow—and, underneath the cart, a shawm blew a nasal fanfare: the timing was so good that it startled even Gabriel. Perhaps the small wooden area with its pulleys and flaps and tricks and

18

traps and splinters and rags was magic, after all.

He saw the tree rise up off the stage and did not see the rope and pulleys that raised it. He began to know how God had felt, looking down on Creation on the seventh day, resting from making the World. It was all very good.

They were three towns away from the Mason. Gabriel had broken his apprentice's bond and no one had hanged him or flogged him or thrown him into prison. In fact the players did not seem to think it was important. They shared their food with him. They gave him a *linen* shirt to wear! And they never mentioned his girlish features or his bush of hair or the fact that he was so small and puny for his age. All they wanted was for him to sit still as a stone—to be a piece of scenery, a decoration like one of the stone angels he had watched the Mason carve, up in the roofs of churches. It was easy.

'Don't pick your nose.'

'Don't scratch.'

'Don't yawn.'

'Don't fidget.'

'Don't go to sleep.'

It was so simple, however hard Izzie tried to make it sound difficult with all her 'don'ts'. Perhaps she did not realize how easy it was to sit perfectly still while you studied the faces one by one of the people in the audience, imagining their names, learned the words of the speaking players, and then—best of all!—played the Wishing Game. He saved up the Wishing Game till last, and then he let his imagination loose.

One day the players would drive through country-side that looked dimly familiar. They would set up the stage among buildings he felt he somehow knew. The audience would gather, one particular yeoman turning aside, out of curiosity, to see these strange outsiders everyone was talking about. The yeoman's wife would tussle for a good place to set down her stool. The

19

chatter would die away. The music would start. Then, seeing the hinged clouds fold down to reveal God and all His angels, the wife would look once and look again and stand up and point and clutch her apron to her mouth . . . And the people round about would tug at her and shout, 'Sit down, Missus!' But she would refuse and say, 'But it's *Gabriel*. It's my Gabriel! Father! Look up yonder. It's our Gabriel and he's an *angel*!'

He would not wave when his mother spotted him. He would just smile and dip his head a little, and she would have to wait until the very end to be reunited with him. They would see how still he could sit!

Why shouldn't it happen? More extraordinary things had happened! One month ago, each new day had lain in wait to ambush Gabriel: he had woken up cringing. Now he was fed and clothed just for sitting still, and crowds looked at him and sighed—'Aaaah!' There was nothing to be afraid of, except perhaps Lucie. (No-one who looked so evil could be quite safe.) But Garvey had a big, round, jolly face. Gabriel could shelter in God's good grace.

Such a weight of worry and terror and contempt had been lifted off his shoulders that he sometimes thought, when the end-music started up beneath the wagon and the audience began to toss like a field of corn, that he could spread his arms, if he wanted, and soar off his ledge, above their heads and round the church tower. As free as a bird. By the time he reached the bottom of the ladder, he was almost laughing out loud with happiness.

'What's so funny?' said Lucifer's daughter (whose job it was to foot the ladder).

'Do you never want to be one of the players, Izzie?' said Gabriel.

She shot him a glance which made him sorry for asking. 'Me? Haven't I got enough to do without learning words?'

'But I don't say any words!' exclaimed Gabriel. 'And you're so clever. You do all kinds of things.'

For a moment, the scowl lifted entirely off Izzie's face, and she looked suddenly very pretty and much younger. She breathed in to say something, but her father came round the corner of the stage. 'She's a girl though, isn't she, Gabriel? You don't have girl players. I mean, I've made her look as much like a boy as I can so she can play her pipe, but there's a limit to how much you can cheat the public. People wouldn't stand for it. Come with me, boy.'

The scowl settled back on to Izzie's forehead. She bustled away again, harassed and busy. Lucie slough-ed his snake's skin and padded into the church building alongside this particular stage, with Gabriel's wrist in one hand. Such a long, bony hand. Gabriel shivered in that grip and in the cold air inside the church. But when he looked back over his shoulder for help, Garvey too had descended his ladder and was following them into the nave. It would be all right if God was there.

'Can you sing, boy?' said Lucie.

'Sing, sir? In church?'

Was it a temptation? Was Lucie tempting him, to see if he would sin, like King David in the Bible who danced and sang in church? Gabriel looked at Garvey for advice. Garvey only nodded and said, 'Go on, son. Sing.'

'Sing, sir? Like the monks?'

'However you like. Just sing.'

So Gabriel sang the first thing that came into his head—loudly:

'*Summer is a-coming in*
Loudly sing cuckoo!
Groweth seed and bloweth mead
And spring the woods anew
Sing cuckoo! Sing cuckoo!'

21

'Holy Jesus and Mary, he's terrible,' said Garvey.

Gabriel suddenly remembered the words of the second verse, and breathed in to begin it. But Garvey clapped a hand over his mouth. 'Never mind, boy. You do a grand job of sitting still.'

He looked disparagingly at Lucie who shrugged and said, 'It was just an idea.'

When they went back outside, Izzie had almost finished packing away the props. It was one of her jobs.

CHAPTER THREE

THE GUILDSMEN

IT WAS the week before the Feast of Corpus Christi when the Mystery wagons rolled into Greathaven, on the east coast. The local dialect was strong; Garvey had difficulty in making a passer-by understand that he wanted to speak to a parish councillor or the Bishop. A bad beginning. But they did not have to search far for the Bishop's secretary: as soon as he saw the pageant wagon, he bore down on it.

The Bishop's secretary was small and sleek like a mole, with padded compartments in his clothes for the precious books he carried with him everywhere—an accounting book and a psalter. Their weight was such that the seam of his coat gaped behind his neck, his shoulders were bowed, and his front hem trailed on the ground. He walked with a teeter, as though he was in the middle of falling on his nose, and brandished a glass lens on a stick as a warning to those in his way that his eyesight was not of the best. He never thought to look through the lens.

'We are travelling players, sir,' said Garvey with his God-like smile.

'Mummers? Jack-o'-Greens? Pagan riff-raff. The Bishop won't stand for it. Paganism in the city. Except on May Day, and that's once too often for me!'

'Not mummers, sir. Tellers of the Mysteries, from the *Creation of the World* to *Doomsday* itself,' said Lucie peaceably. 'Also the miracles of the holy saints and their Mother in Heaven, the Blessed Virgin, as lately performed in French churches . . .'

'Morris dancers and mudwater-medicine merchants!' mouthed the Bishop's secretary, jabbing his eyeglass in the playmaster's face. 'The Mysteries, did you say? Don't you think we've got Mysteries of our own? Don't you think our own townsmen can put on a Corpus Christi play? What? Think you're bringing Christianity to the heathens, do you? Who sent you? Who's your Bishop? French did you say?'

Garvey began pompously: 'Sir, the Mysteries of . . . of . . .'

('Greathaven,' Lucie prompted.)

'The Mysteries of Greathaven are famed even in the far distant streets of my own home town . . .'

'Now I know you're charlatans!' crowed the secretary triumphantly. 'The Guilds have not put on a Mystery here these five years or more!'

'Ah, then . . .'

'But they *might* this year!' interrupted the secretary. 'You're not wanted here. Take yourselves off!'

Garvey was losing patience. 'Damn me. You're one week off Corpus Christi. Surely you know if your Guildsmen are rehearsing a Mystery, man!'

Lucie sucked in air through his teeth. He could see from the changing mottle of the secretary's complexion that Garvey had made up his mind for him. He would refuse them permission for a play.

'You'll get no permission from my Bishop for your scurvy play till I've examined the script word by word.'

'We have no script, sir. We have the lines by heart. We've not a reading man among us,' said Lucie dejectedly.

'No script? No scholars? You shouldn't be allowed to represent the Bible and God's holy saints. And you won't in this town. I won't so much as put your petition in front of my Bishop. I wouldn't waste his time on you. He's a busy man. Away with you and your mumming!'

'Well? Do we play for pennies, without the Bishop's permission?' said Garvey.

Lucie looked doubtful. 'If that otter sees us collecting money . . .' But it was obvious he was tempted. To put on a play in a town which had let its Mysteries lapse for five years—it was a serious temptation.

Garvey made a show of waiting for Lucie's opinion, but his mind was already made up. 'I say we give them *Balaam and His Ass*—just you, me and the boy—and be very discreet gathering their farthings. That little pine-martin doesn't frighten me.'

It was a strange, small, unambitious play about a man and his donkey who encounter an angel. The donkey can see the angel but the rider cannot. Garvey was to take the part of Balaam, and Lucie his donkey. But it seemed Lucie had lost a lot of weight since the last time they had played it. The weight of Garvey on his narrow, bony shoulders, combined with the close fit of the donkey-head, seemed to cause him some distress, because he suddenly reeled up against a wall and snatched off the head. His cheeks were sallow and sucked into the hollows between his teeth. Garvey's leg was scraped against the wall, and he got down complaining. They changed roles, and Lucie climbed up on the playmaster's shoulders, his weight hardly bending Garvey's back.

Here was Gabriel's chance to leave his wooden perch and to stand stage-centre with a huge property sword as tall as himself. Feet splayed, shoulders back, all he had to do was to look ethereal, wield his sword, and remember one verse of poetry. So he did not understand why Izzie touched him on the shoulder before they began and said, 'At the first sign of any

25

trouble, just stop. Right?' Her frown was worse than ever.

A little crowd gathered readily enough. When he went on, Gabriel drew a spectacular sigh from all the women watching. The clowning of Balaam and the donkey soon had them hooting and pointing and calling out to Balaam: 'An angel! An angel! Can't you see?' A boy sitting on a wall fell off backwards and came running round the end of the wall a moment later saying, 'What have I missed? What have I missed!'

Gabriel stood, feet apart, shoulders back, his outstretched hands resting on the hilt of the big tin sword. He practised his lines over and over again inside his head until his lips began to move as he repeated them. Balaam whipped on his donkey. The donkey threw its rider to the ground in a dozen different, hilarious ways. Once it threw Lucie halfway across the stage, and he landed on his back at Gabriel's feet. It was so funny. Gabriel had to bite his cheeks to keep from bursting out laughing. Then he saw the look on Lucie's face, the long strip of sweat down the centre of his shirt, and realized that he was not enjoying himself, and that Garvey was. It did not seem funny after that. And when Gabriel saw Izzie's cropped head turn away from the stage, her hands over her eyes, he suddenly wished the play was over.

Some of the audience had stopped laughing, too, but not out of pity for Lucie. The ones who had stopped were looking over their shoulders at a cordon of men drifting in twos and threes out of the side streets and doorways and converging on the play. Some of the women in the audience gathered up their skirts and left at once. Gabriel's eye was drawn by the movement. It broke his concentration. Some of the men were carrying axes or mallets.

Gabriel looked across at Izzie. But she still had her eyes hidden against seeing her father thrown across the stage. He looked out across the audience again: the men were almost shoulder-to-shoulder now, across the street. He could recognize their trades from the clothes they were wearing—dyers, carpenters, wheelwrights, masons, stevedores up from the docks, and several cordwainers: the spikes in their hands looked like daggers.

'Gabriel,' said Lucie in a low whisper. He had to say it twice. 'Gabriel. Say your lines.'

'Oh!' squeaked Gabriel.

> 'ForshameBalaamthou foolishclown
> whothinkstorideanangeldown,
> yourlowlybeast,yourhumblemule
> hasshownmorereverencethanyou
>   . . . Oh

Master, help!'

Lucie stared up at him from the plank floor, his eyebrows twitching with dismay. He followed the direction of the boy's wild-eyed stare.

The Guildsmen were wading through the audience, overturning benches and chasing children away with the backs of their hands. Grasping the situation immediately, Lucie rose to his feet and half-carried, half-pushed Gabriel over the back of the cart. 'Izzie! Find somewhere safe!' Then he turned, his hands outspread, as the Guildsmen reached the front of the stage. The audience had melted away entirely.

'What harm?' said Lucie, turning on his demon's smile. 'What harm, gentlemen. I understood the Mysteries weren't played here any more. Our most heartfelt apologies if we were mistaken. In any case, this isn't a Mystery. It's nothing! Just a half-hour's entertainment! How can something so mean cast a shadow over your own magnificent efforts as actors of a Guild Mystery? Why, I've heard tell from the Bishop's secretary that yours used to be the best

Mystery in the land, bar none. We might even stay to see it and learn from it ourselves . . . that's if you are performing on Corpus Christi Day. What are we? Only a band of poor Christians, same as you, shining a light on God's holy word in the language God planted in our mouths. Take a seat, lads, and let us show you a sample of our poor . . .'

A cordwainer drove his marlin-spike into the platform between Lucie's feet. The Guildsmen put their shoulders against the side of the cart, and began rocking it. The flat rear scenery broke its guy rope and crashed forward, so that Garvey and Lucie had to jump off the cart and into the arms of the hostile tradesmen. Izzie, who had hidden Gabriel in a barrel once again and was about to climb into one herself, jumped down and ran towards the crowd shouting, 'Leave them alone! Don't you dare hurt them!'

Gabriel popped up out of his barrel to see the brawl which was just beginning when suddenly everyone froze, as if a wizard had cast a spell over them. Down the street came the cry, 'Peace! On pain of my displeasure!'

The Bishop of Greathaven was as stately as a ship heaving landward. His small, glistening secretary plunged along in front of him like a dolphin under the bowsprit. A handbell in the Bishop's fist clanged like a ship's bell.

'Riotous rabble! Riotous rabble!' boomed the Bishop. Birds took off in alarm from the rooftops. The Guildsmen leapt out of his path, trying at the same time to bend a reverent knee. The Bishop did not slow his stride until he came face to face with Garvey. 'You see where your ill-manners have led you, man? What did you think you were doing? Did I give you my blessing? No! Did the council sponsor you? No! Well? Justify yourself, man, if you are able!'

'. . . just a poor band of Christians . . .' Garvey mumbled.

28

'And you!' The Bishop turned his back on Garvey to address his flock. 'Justify yourself, John the Dyer!'

'Well . . . outsiders putting on a Mystery . . . it's for men of the Guilds . . . local men . . . these strangers and foreigners . . . stealing our glory . . .' His excuses petered out and he hung his head shamedly.

'How did you hope to profit?' The Bishop had turned his bellowing wrath on Lucie.

'Who, me, holy Father?' He seemed dazed, and one eye was closing after a punch or a fall on stage.

So his daughter loyally started to say, 'We were going to pass a purse around . . .'

Lucie raised his voice to drown hers. 'No profit, father. We must follow our calling even when there's none to pay us. No profit in mind, holy Father. We were playing for purest charity.'

The Bishop held up one authoritative hand. 'It is a piteous shame that you did not have the civility to ask my permission. I would willingly have sponsored a Corpus Christi Mystery, being so close to the Feast-day.' (The players looked to the secretary, waiting for him to speak. But he only smirked at them maliciously and kept silent.) 'Secretary! Tell the Constable to lock up these vagrants overnight—the whole pack of them. That may teach them not to beg. And in the morning, gentlemen, I would advise you to turn your backs on Greathaven.'

'As Lot turned his back on Sodom, your highness,' said Lucie. 'As Moses turned his back on the Red Sea. As . . .'

'That's enough, player. Surrender yourself to the lock-up before I recommend a longer stay . . . Oh, and Secretary—don't overlook the boy hiding in that barrel over there! Now . . . a blessing on each townsman who goes directly home.'

With a quantity of black looks and complaints, the Guildsmen shuffled away towards their homes, and the Bishop blessed them as they went. The players shambled silently up the main street to the lock-up—a small, six-sided shed in the middle of the crossroads. There they had to wait some time until the Constable could find the key and lock the door on them. The Sexton's pig had wandered in while the lock-up was not in use, and given birth to a litter of six piglets. The players sat as far away from her as they could, but the smell and the squealing promised to keep them awake all night.

Lucie let go an involuntary groan and slumped against the wall with his head in his hands. Izzie glowered at Garvey through the thickening darkness. 'Did you have to throw him down so hard?' She went to link her hands sympathetically through Lucie's arm, but her father snatched his arm away, whining in a sarcastic, piping voice, '"We were going to pass a purse around!" What a fool! It's your fault we're here. It's your words got us locked up for begging. You're worse shame to me than udders on a bull. Don't you go trying to put the blame on the Master. You know what we'll find in the morning—and all thanks to you, my girl.'

In his corner of the cell Gabriel, overwhelmed by the shame of prison and the nearness of the pig, clutched his knees to his chest and rocked to and fro, trying to imagine he was somewhere else. His imagination deserted him. When Izzie came and sat next to him, she seemed close to crying. He nestled up against her and whispered sympathetically, 'He's evil, isn't he? I hate him, too.'

'Who?' she said, sniffing quietly.

'Your father, of course!'

Izzie snatched her arm from between his hands and snapped. 'Oh shut your mouth, boy. You don't understand anything. You stupid boy!'

Early in the morning, the pig and piglets were asleep, but Adam and Eve were stirring. Gabriel woke to see their two heads silhouetted against the bars in

30

the door. They were speaking to Lucie. 'Sorry, but we've done arguing. John and Simon are going, too, soon as the door's open. They just hadn't the stomach to tell you so themselves. This is no way to carry on. The tide's against the Mysteries. They're finished.'

'And you rats are leaving the ship before it sinks,' hissed Lucie. 'Who else? How many are left when the deserters are gone?'

Adam sighed. 'None, Lucie. A couple of musicians, that's all. It's finished. Can't you see? If they start locking up players for vagrants, then clearly the country lays no store by its Mysteries. All right. They were good. We remember them when we were children. They were merry. But those days are gone. Just like the Druids: we've outlived our time.'

'But the words, man! *The Words*! People rise up and die, but the words should go on!' The whole cell rustled as Lucie's raised voice disturbed the sleeping. The pig grunted.

Eve spat through the bars and rubbed at the stubble of his beard aggressively. 'Lord, how you carp on, Lucie. I don't know why you never learned yourself to write your precious *words*. Words aren't coins in your pocket. You can't spend them. You should have learned reading and writing, then you wouldn't make life a misery for the likes of us.'

'Damn you, you traitor! You Judas!' shouted the devil-man, and all the piglets woke up with a start and hurtled round the lock-up colliding with prisoners and shrieking like souls in torment: a blitz of piglets.

It was mid-morning before the Constable remembered them and came to unbolt the lock-up. Adam and Eve, John and Simon never even went back to the site of the play. They turned towards the sea and went to look for work on the boats. When the rest got back to the pageant carts, local Guildsmen had been there before them. They had come in the night and lit a fire under the stage.

31

All that remained were four smoking wheelhubs, thirty-six metal rims off the barrels, and two nervous horses. They found Lucifer's tail hanging in a tree and the donkey's head jammed on a gatepost. It looked as if it was laughing at them.

CHAPTER FOUR

THE MIRACLE

WHEN THE worst thing has happened that can happen, a certain kind of relief sets in. Hob and Jack said goodbye and went down to the boats too. Garvey managed to exchange one horse for a small cart, in which the 'company' could travel on. The musicians, Rolande and Ydrys, stayed. They had taken their instruments with them to the lock-up. So they were able still to play doleful airs as they and Lucie and Izzie and Gabriel all bounced about, knee to knee, in the cart. Garvey drove.

The road was too rough for one thought to rest long in mind before it was cannoned out by another. In the end, Gabriel's head was shaken vacant, and he sat gaping ahead of him into Izzie's scowling face and listening to his teeth clattering together with every rut in the road.

There was a thick mist lying on the track which ran through flat, tedious marshland. A bittern-bird was booming across the flats—an eerie, human sound. Lucie's blacked eye was tight closed, and he seemed to take particularly unkindly to the bumps.

'Are you all right, Father?' said Izzie.

'I am.'

'Shall we ever put on a play again, do you think?'

'It would take a miracle.' He replied in a clipped, matter-of-fact voice, with a hint of blame in it.

'That's just the kind I was talking about,' said Garvey over his shoulder.

'No!' snapped Lucie. 'You won't get me mixing in that kind of thing.'

Gabriel nodded eagerly to himself. He had been quite right about the devil-man. Lucie did not even like the mention of miracles. So Lucie would not pray for one. Gabriel bowed his own head and dashed off a prayer, trying not to let his knees touch against Lucie's. Just as he finished, Garvey stood up and hauled on the reins. The cart shuddered to a halt. A wail more dismal than the bird cries rose up from under the horse.

'God have mercy, I'm done for!'

'Get out of the road, you old fool, or I'll run you down.'

'Didn't you already do that, you son of Cain you?' said the voice.

'What manner of place is that to be lying down, then, you mangy ferret?'

'Peaceful as a churchyard, but I didn't think to be making my grave in it!'

'Don't you know it's an offence to lie down on the King's highway and make yourself a danger to passing traffic?'

'Well, and is it you with all the hoof-prints up and down his back, master lawyer? The smallest thing you could do would be to help a poor injured man towards the comfort of an inn!'

'Flim-flam! If your legs are broken, walk on your hands!' bellowed Garvey.

'Come down out of your chariot, Queen Boadicea and I'll show you . . .'

'You'll regret you said that!' And Garvey jumped down and was swallowed up immediately by the fuming mist.

Gabriel knelt up inside the cart and peered out to see what would happen. He thought how poisonous

34

these mists must be that rolled in over the east coast: all the local inhabitants were as aggressive as fighting cocks. It was a wonder they had not all mauled each other to death long ago and left the damp, chilly coastline unpeopled except for howling birds.

The mist was as white and solid and damp as a giant wet sheep crossing the road. It smothered both Garvey and the foot-traveller. Lucie began to look nervously around for fear it was part of an ambush by footpads. 'Garvey was a fool to get down,' he muttered.

They were gone a long time. The mist stifled all sounds except for the distant sea. Or was it the marsh-grass hissing, acre upon salt-caked acre? There were no grunts, no thumps, no scuffling of feet. Then the mists heaved and Garvey reappeared, his arm round the traveller's shoulders and that great generous smile beaming into the stranger's face. 'We're taking my friend here as far as Horsey. He'll ride up beside me.'

The stranger's face was almost hidden by a leather cap tied on with a strip of canvas. It pinched his features together and bunched them round his bulbous nose. But Gabriel caught one glimpse of milky-white eyes that looked stone blind.

The foot-traveller shared the driving-board with Garvey, their elbows and heads pressed close together all the way into Horsey, and their voices murmuring.

It was not much of a town—hardly more than a village. They put the stranger down on the outskirts and left him standing in the middle of the road, his face in shadow under his cap and just a glimmer of those white, pebbly eyes.

'What's it to be, then?' said Garvey, striding away from the cart and putting a hand on Gabriel's head. One side of the cart had been cut away and a plank balanced in front, on carpenter's trestles loaned free and willingly. Horsey was a friendly place. To further extend the stage, they established themselves alongside the fuller's house where the broad stone steps of an outside staircase climbed the side of the building to a loft door—a ready-made Hill of Heaven.

'What's it to be, then. Gabriel shall choose.'

'Not *Balaam and his Ass*!' Izzie blurted out. 'Father's not fit enough.'

'I said it was Gabriel's choice, *madam*. You're getting too much mouth on you for one as doesn't earn her keep. What about it, Gabriel my son? A speaking part. You were good in Greathaven. You remembered your lines.'

Izzie grimaced at Gabriel from behind the playmaster's back, and shook her head. 'I like *Noah*,' said Gabriel.

'Oh, an excellent choice, lad! But unfortunately all the animal masks got burned in the fire. Except for the donkey. And all our actors have taken themselves off and deserted our little pageant, see? Myself, I'd like to see you take another try at *Balaam*.'

Gabriel turned so that Izzie could not catch his eye. He did not want to be difficult. He wanted to do what the Master wanted. He nodded his head.

'Well done! And because you remembered your lines so well, I'll maybe give you a verse or two more to learn. Let me see now.' He hooked a finger into the corner of his mouth, as though he was versifying on the spot. But the words came out just as if Garvey had spent all morning thinking about them. Gabriel thought it astonishing.

> 'Thy donkey here is wiser far
> Who stopped so full of reverent fear
> When lovesome God did send me here
> To bar the road.
> Now ope' thine eyes, thou dotterel
> And see what is invisible—

The holy angel Gabriel
Sent from God's abode!

Think, son, you'll be the first actor ever to speak the lines!'

Lucie gave a deep groan and slapped the side of his head. 'I see the way of it. That's the end. Finish. If that's the way you're going, Izzie and I are clearing off.'

'The choice is yours, old friend.' Garvey beamed cheerfully. 'Needs must. A pageant costs money. I need money more than I need you. Stay if you like, go if you choose.'

'But you don't know half the words he does!' Izzie protested.

'Where will his precious words be without a pageant cart to spout them on?' Garvey retorted, grinning. (At least, his teeth were bared.)

'Anywhere! What does a piece of painted wood matter?' Lucie made a lunge for Gabriel's wrist and pulled at him. 'Are you going to be a party to this, boy?'

'What?'

'He doesn't understand, Father,' said Izzie.

Garvey caught Gabriel's other wrist. 'But he knows I always do what's best for everyone—don't you, son?'

For a moment or two, the men hauled on Gabriel like a soul on the Day of Judgement fought over by angels and devils. There was no contest. Gabriel looked up into the two faces: there was Garvey, curl-haired, jolly, with a shining bald tonsure and round, red cheeks, bright blue eyes and long, dark lashes; and there was Lucie, his skin stretched so tight over his bones that its yellowness might have been the skull shining through; deep-hollowed eyes and troughs under his cheek-bones like two gouges of the Mason's chisel; and those flashing, foreign eyes. There was no

37

contest. Gabriel twisted his hand out of Lucie's grip and ran to shelter behind Garvey. Izzie glared at him with the same dark, foreign eyes as her father's. Garvey ruffled his angel's hair affectionately. 'There's my good, sensible friend.'

So the play went ahead in Horsey. But Lucie stayed after all, to play Balaam, and Izzie to play her pipe beforehand. For just when Gabriel thought he was rid of the devil-man, he saw them arguing at a distance, father and daughter; Izzie pointing back towards the cart, Lucie shaking his head; Izzie tugging on his arm, pleading, and her father pushing her away. Gabriel found himself whispering, 'Let him go and you stay, Izzie. Let him go and *you* stay.' He had not realized before that he would miss her.

Both father and daughter returned. When Izzie did not come to fluff out Gabriel's hair and tie the laces of his shirt before the performance, he thought she must be angry with him and he was sorry. But the playmaster himself came to look him over and turn him about and about, examining him through narrowed eyes and hearing over his lines. 'Whatever happens, son, go on looking holy and don't say a word more than I told you. Got that? I'm relying on you, friend.'

Three times Balaam tried to drive his donkey along the desert road. Three times his donkey saw the invisible angel sent by God, and stopped dead. But Garvey and Lucie had to clown more than before. The audience were slower to laugh themselves into such a roaring mirth. They were unsettled at the start by a blind man pushing his way to the middle of the audience, barking out 'Make way! Make way for a poor blind man.' Gabriel, standing motionless, his feet apart, shoulders back and hands resting on the sword-hilt, caught sight of the man out of the corner of his eye. It was a strange sight: a blind man at a spectacle.

Again and again, the playmaster threw down his

rider before Lucie, breathless and slow of movement, began his speech demanding to know why the donkey kept stopping. The donkey opened its hairy jaws and said in a braying voice:

'See you not God's angel, there?
Like the sun his blazing hair;
Bright his sword and stern his stare
Forbidding me to pass.'

Lucie's black eyes flickered towards the audience. He moistened his lips, wincing.

'He thinks I won't remember my lines,' thought Gabriel, 'or that I'll rush them like I did last time. I'll show him.' And he launched into his speech.

'For shame, Balaam, you foolish clown,
Who thinks to ride an angel down!
Your lowly beast, your humble mule,
Has shown more reverence than you!
I bring a message from on high—
'Tis God Himself who speaks, not I!

Thy donkey here is wiser far
Who stopped so full of reverent fear
When lovesome God did send me here
To bar the road.
Now ope' thine eyes, thou dotterel
And see what is invisible—
The holy angel Gabriel
Sent from God's abode!'

'A miracle!' came the cry from the audience. Someone was on his feet, his hands cupped over his eyes. 'The sun! Jesu, how the sun blazes! How the face of God's angel dazzles me! Oh! Oh!'

'Sit down and shut it,' growled two or three men, but the women were crossing themselves already and knocking over their stools in turning round. It was the blind man.

'Twenty years I wandered in darkness! Praise be to God our Father for this holy child. Turn your face on me, miraculous boy, and bless me with another sight of you!'

'I hate this play,' thought Gabriel. 'Something always goes wrong.' Spoiling his grand posture as little as possible, he glanced quickly sideways into the crowd to see who was speaking to whom.

'Oh!' shrieked the blind man. 'Doesn't his holy image singe itself into your very brain? Down on your knees, you godless vermin! Don't you see? God's holy angel is among us! As he spoke the words, my eyes were opened!'

Gabriel blushed violently and felt the sweat spring through his palms and trickle down the hilt of his tin sword. The blind man was pointing at him, his milky-white eyes shivering in their sockets and a smile of radiant joy revealing his rotted teeth.

About half the audience fell to their knees with a clatter of upturned benches. Those left standing looked around sheepishly, as though, like Adam and Eve, they suddenly found they were naked and in the open. Self-consciously they ducked down among the rest.

Garvey had gone to the rim of the stage, his donkey's head under his arm and his pate gleaming with sweat. He pointed at the blind man. 'What did you see, Christian?' He had a look of childish bewilderment on his face.

'I saw the Angel Gabriel, and as God's my witness 'tis the first sight I've seen these twenty-five years! I saw him and I see him still! Hallelujah!'

Gabriel wanted to dive over the back of the stage, as he had to escape the Guildsmen in Greathaven. He looked to the playmaster for help, but Garvey had one hand behind his back, spread as if to say, 'Don't move.' ('Whatever happens, son, don't say a word more than I told you. I'm relying on you.' The words hatched out of Gabriel's memory and teemed through his head, overrunning every other thought.) With the other hand, Garvey was scratching his head in puzzlement. 'To be sure, the lad's name *is* Gabriel, and he came to me the very day I was needing an angel. But what are you telling me, Christian? Let's be very clear. Are you saying that the words of this boy healed your blindness?'

The milky-eyed man was back on his feet, the zeal of his speech fetching him off the ground in little hops and leaps. 'Not his words only, but the image of his golden head burned itself through the scales on my eyes! A shrine! We must raise a shrine to this little angel and bring him tributes. Curse me for having nothing in this world to give him but gratitude!'

'Down on your knees. Show respect,' said Garvey to Lucie, who was leaning against the corner strut of the stage with his eyes fixed on the far horizon. The playmaster flung a friendly arm round his shoulders. But Garvey's fingers went white with the amount of strength he had to apply to get Lucie on his knees. Garvey never once stopped smiling his God-like smile. Gabriel heard Lucie groan as he sank down.

Then Garvey was standing in front of his angel, beaming into his face and murmuring, without moving his lips, 'Don't answer. Into the loft and shut the door behind you 'fore they start wanting to touch. *Tell me lad,*' (Gabriel reeled backwards at the sudden loudness of Garvey's voice) '*tell us all. Did you knowingly work this miracle? Did you restore this man's sight? Can you make the blind see?*'

Gabriel took his hands off the hilt of the sword, expecting it to fall with a clatter. But its tip was jammed between two planks of the stage and it stood up, gently flexing. Gabriel leapt from the stage to the stone steps and slipped into the dark slit of shade where the loft door stood ajar. He closed it with a bang, and stood with his back to it. His heartbeat shook him, like footsteps shaking a hollow, wooden stage.

Ten minutes later, Garvey knocked softly at the door and Gabriel let him in along with Lucie, Izzie and the musicians.

'You did grandly, son,' said the playmaster, barring the door. 'The sword was a grand touch. They had their eyes so fixed on its wagging that some said you'd disappeared in plain sight.'

Gabriel was urgent to know just one thing. 'Can the blind man still see?'

The question seemed to amuse Garvey and disgust the devil-man. After a moment's thought, Garvey said, 'Certainly he can, Gabriel. He's away on a pilgrimage to Walsingham now, to give thanks.' And he threw back his head and laughed so that his whole chest shook.

Everyone else was so quiet, so scowling. Gabriel looked from face to face in search of some explanation. Why were they not astounded, baffled, gasping and wondering? How often had they seen miracles happen in front of their very eyes? He felt he ought to understand. He felt ignorant. 'It *was* a miracle, wasn't it, though?' he asked in a whisper.

Lucie groaned again. Izzie threw out her hands towards him in an expression of exasperation. 'Are you stupid or what? Of course it . . .'

From behind her, Garvey cupped Izzie's small jaw in one hand, turning her face over her shoulder and towards his. 'What's this? What's this? Not a doubting Thomas, I hope? You know what happens to unbelievers when they die, don't you Lizabette. You know how they fast in everlasting fire, and how devils tear out their mischievous tongues. Where's your faith, *little girl*. Don't you know that faith can move mountains and build pageants out of gold and silver?'

Lucie came and drew his daughter away into the total darkness of the loft. His voice boomed startlingly out of the pitch black. 'And haven't you heard the Scriptures saying that a man should tie a millstone round his neck and throw himself in the sea sooner than abuse a little child?'

That night, sleeping on the draughty slab floor of the fuller's loft, without supper or a blanket, Gabriel's dreams were an avalanche of frightening pictures. He dreamt that Lucie threw him from the parapet of a bridge into deep water, with a stone statue of Garvey tied round his neck. Down and down the weight dragged him, to where strange fish swam past and gaped at him with milky, quivering eyes. A silver fish-hook tangled in his curls, dangled by Izzie, and when he woke she was tugging gently on his hair. Her head was close up against him, her mouth against his ear. 'Don't trust him, Gabriel. Don't believe Garvey. It was all a hoax.' She slithered away on her stomach across the slatted floor, just like her father moved when he played the serpent in the Garden of Eden.

In the morning, Gabriel could not be sure whether she had been there or not. He suspected she was just another image from his dream-packed sleep.

At the foot of the outside staircase, their forlorn little wagon looked somehow festive. Ribbons had been tied to the charred remains of the weather-vane. A pair of slippers were balanced on the rim of the stage, alongside a keg of beer and two huge loaves of bread. A lamb's fleece was sprawled in the middle of the stage.

Standing at the top of the steps, Gabriel held out his hand, thinking to feel rain. But what he had taken at first for raindrops on the wagon floor were actually pennies, halfpennies and farthings scattered everywhere. In a leather purse hung on the handle of the loft door were eight bright shillings.

Lucie, Izzie, the musicians and the playmaster set

about gathering up the presents without a word. 'Are they really for us?' said Gabriel. They backed the horse between the traces and untied her hobble, without a glance at the Horsey townsfolk who watched them from a very great distance. Gabriel remained standing at the top of the steps: Garvey told him to do so. When the cart was ready, he called Gabriel to sit beside him on the driver's bench. All he said, as they drew out of the village, was, 'Next off, we must get you a pair of wings, my son.'

CHAPTER FIVE

THE PRIDE OF PEACOCKS

GABRIEL DID get a pair of wings made from filigree wire quilted with the tips of peacock feathers. He did not wear them: they were nailed to the scenery above where he sat, like an immense butterfly impaled against the wood. In the sunlight they glowed an iridescent purple, green and turquoise—a thousand eyes gazing over his shoulders. He had a white satin shirt, too, and a long red velvet coat.

Velvet. He sat and watched it fall into folds across his knee and the dense depth of its scarlet pile was more delightful than wine or the blood from roasting beef. 'If Squit could see me now!'

A hammered metal disc was fastened between his peacock wings, to serve as a halo behind his head. It could be angled to catch the sun and create a dazzle which, on a sunny day, made the Angel Gabriel a thing too bright to look upon. He was encouraged by Garvey to polish it, but would have done so anyway: he had never before owned a mirror. Back in the bad days, working for the Mason, his reflection in a church window or a bowl of washing water had stared out at him like an evil spirit—all girlish, sheepish, wimpish. He would cloud it with his breath or splash it to pieces with his hands. Had he changed so much, then, since that time? Not at all. Except that he ate venison and roast lamb, and drank milk laced with honey, or hot mead fragrant with herbs. As a result,

45

his skin glowed more healthily and his halo of hair gleamed like the outer circle of the sun.

He was not often given words to speak, and had only to sit in the shade of his massive wings and stare into the middle distance and drift in his imagination to the four corners of the sky. News of the pageant reached every village ahead of them. A place was always ready for it. The crowd was always bigger than the crowd before. The takings reached sums past Gabriel's imagining.

Until Garvey bought a pair of horses, pedestrians followed them, walking alongside the cart. Gabriel was not permitted to show himself, and had to duck down inside the cart, underneath the costumes.

They paused for a while in the Welsh marches, where Garvey commissioned the building of a pageant. The like of it never has nor ever will be seen again. It stood twenty-five spans high and took four horses to pull it. The stage had a hollow depth of eight spans, enough for fireworks and twelve costume changes to be stored. The Mouth of Hell gaped with cowhide jowls and bellows in the throat to expel the yellow smoke. The Hill of Heaven was flowery with silk blooms and the tree from the Garden of Eden was discarded in favour of a glittering cloth-of-gold pavilion perfect for transformation scenes and disappearing tricks. The new weather-vane was a gold-leaf cockerel with streamers of silver. It was too heavy to turn in the wind, but it mattered little to know which way the wind was blowing: wherever it blew it blew word of the miraculous pageant and the Angel Gabriel.

Competition to join the troupe was murderous. Guildsmen versed in all the Mystery plays from the *Creation of the World* to *Doomsday* clamoured to travel with Garvey. He turned down all but a handful—'the handful who came with their hands full,' said Lucie, meaning that they bribed their way in.

None of their skill was needed. Those who had

never acted in Guild Mysteries were just as likely to be accepted as those who had all the verses committed to memory. Few of the old words were spoken. The repertory was small, consisting of any Mystery where an angel played an important part. And these were performed mostly as mimes, for fear Gabriel should be overburdened with the learning of words.

When Lucie suggested they should play others of the Mysteries, Garvey would say, 'Where's the angel in that?'

'There's no call for an angel,' the devil-man would mutter malevolently. 'Nor room for miracles, either.'

Gabriel came to the conclusion that Lucie was jealous of the red velvet and the peacock feathers.

All that was generally required of Gabriel was to point a finger, or spread his arms; to stand up majestically, or fling himself forward into a flying harness high above the stage. He rarely paid any attention to the plays progressing below him. They were ponderous and unfunny, and never reached an end before some new miracle in the audience brought the crowds milling round the stage, shouting and pushing and throwing gifts. They swept forward like a sea-wave, and left a litter of presents and tributes along the rim of the stage. If the village priest tried to intervene (as some did), he would be overrun, trampled, cursed by the crowd. But more often, he was there in the front row with a chalice or a chasuble to lay on the stage.

An audience never failed to gasp and cry out when Gabriel flung himself into the flying harness, arms outstretched and billowing with silk. (Strangely, Gabriel never felt he could fly when he was wearing the harness. He thought them rather silly for not understanding how the trick was worked.)

But the miracles never failed to amaze him. Sometimes a woman knotted up with arthritis like a ship's rope would throw up her gnarled hands and swear that her pain was gone. A young woman with her hands clapped over her head would say that her headache had flown away on wings, like a butterfly. An old man with only one eye said that he saw the Virgin Mary standing behind Gabriel, dressed in purple and green. The lame walked. The deaf heard. The dumb spoke. Childless women declaimed prayers to the Virgin in Latin while tears rolled down their faces; and the parents of idiot children danced with them in the market place, swearing that their little brains had been set all to rights. Gabriel had never realized how many sick or imperfect people there were in the world.

A lidded box was nailed to the side of the cart where the scholarly or the rich could post written petitions for miracles.

'What do they say?' asked Gabriel after one performance.

'Who knows?' replied Garvey, chortling as he threw the petitions one by one into the dark interior of the cart. 'Who can read?'

Gabriel couldn't. Out of curiosity, he caught one as it flew past his head, broke the wax seal, and unrolled the paper. But the jumble of letters only looked like a chorus of angels skipping hand in hand across the sheet. 'I ought to know,' said Gabriel, doggedly staring at the writing. 'How can I do a miracle if I don't know what they're asking for?'

The busy movements of the players, packing the pageant for the road, all ebbed to a halt. Garvey stopped grinning and his eyes turned on Gabriel. Lucie threw down the cup he was holding and drove it into the mud with his foot. As Izzie dredged it up again, her growing hair flopped forward over her face and hid what she was thinking. Gabriel blushed and wondered why everyone was looking at him. Normally they paid him no attention between performances. Garvey broke the silence.

48

'Quite right. You're absolutely right, Gabriel. Some day soon we'll stop by at a monastery and have a scribbler read them out to you. How does that suit you?'

Gabriel nodded solemnly and went back to stroking the red velvet of his costume and eating an apple. The responsibilities of being an angel sometimes weighed on him. 'Why is it that everybody doesn't get better?' he wondered out loud.

Garvey was quick with his answer. 'Miracles take time, little lad. Perhaps they're not completed until after we leave town.'

'Ah!' Gabriel smiled and felt much better. It was good to think of all those sick people gradually recovering as the pageant rolled off over their horizon. He had a mental picture of the country hanging like a broken web between the branching sea, and the pageant travelling, like an industrious spider, to every tear in turn, patching and mending the damage. One day the whole population would be perfect and shining again under the silver dewfall. It was a miraculous feeling—as though his soul had been crammed over-large inside his chest and was struggling to expand. He was strong, he was powerful, he was *special*. He climbed the ladder and studied his face for half an hour in the silver disc that was his halo. At the end, he looked down and called out to Lucie, 'You there! Fetch me another apple!'

The devil-man crossed the stage with his loping, thief-like walk and took an apple half-eaten out of the fist of another player. Then he leaned back from his narrow hips and hurled the apple directly at Gabriel's head. It missed, shattering damply against the silver halo. 'Take heed from the Fall of Lucifer, brat! It was pride in his beauty that was his undoing!'

On and on they travelled, rattling appallingly fast over

the rutted roads so as to outstrip the pilgrims who followed them out of each town and village. Gabriel took to sitting on the cart-tail and waving to them; it seemed so ungrateful to speed away from their flattery and blessings. Lucie saw him wave and pointed a jeering finger, saying aside to his daughter, 'Yah, look at the little Pope blessing the faithful!'

Gabriel's hand froze in mid-air and he blushed scarlet. But then he began to wave again, muttering to himself, 'He's just jealous of my velvet.'

Izzie never came near or spoke to Gabriel. The pageant was so big that they could keep far apart from each other without trying. And besides, there was soon a property wagon and two more sleeping wagons for the many members of the wealthy company. Gabriel always slept under the stage, however, wrapped in a massively expensive duckdown quilt, because Garvey was anxious he should not catch cold.

His body had never known such kindness. It was almost as if he had no body, because no part of it hurt, or itched, or shivered with cold, or even felt the wooden planking through the quilt. It was bliss. It was like being a spirit in the Realm of Bliss. No wonder the angels praised God. Gabriel praised God from top to tail of his eiderdown, and glorified God's servant Garvey who snored inside his own duckdown quilt, at the other end of the darkness.

The streets of Pontydd were deserted as the pageant rolled through. All of its people were waiting on a glebe meadow outside their cramped little town. There did not seem to be a living soul left among the houses, except for someone banging on the door of the lock-up. 'Let me out! Unloose me, you pack of devil-worshippers! I forbid this thing! I forbid it! Let me out unless the fires of Hell daunt you not at all! There'll be no forgiveness. No, not for one man, woman or child. There'll be penances, too, in plenty!'

Garvey stopped the pageant and went to peer

through the grille. A hand reached out and snatched at his head. 'Who's that? Unbolt this door, if you're a Christian. In the name of all the saints, I conjure you to open this door, or the whole town will be in the hands of the Devil by nightfall!'

'Why's that?' said Garvey, slapping the hands that groped between the iron bars.

'Where are you from? Haven't you heard? It's the miracle-madness—those travelling bandits with their gilded snares to catch the ignorant and the innocent. I'm the priest of this town. In all the days of my life I've never seen such a rebellion against God's will— nor against his appointed ministers. Angel? Miracle-worker? It's a strumpet out of Hell stealing away their money and their souls! Dear brother, let me out of this awful place and the blessed Virgin will reward you. So will I! We can purge this disease from the countryside!'

'Ah, now you're speaking my language, wester-man,' said Garvey, gaily drawing back the bolt. 'Reward did you say?'

The priest burst out of the lock-up, shielding his eyes against the bright sunlight. As he uncovered them, he was confronted with the pageant, its gold and silverwork dazzling in the sunshine, and the weathercock gracefully bowing to the north in the breeze. Lined up alongside it was the company, shoulder to shoulder and silent. The empty peacock wings blazed like purple fire at the top of the gantry. The priest saw a boy of astonishing personal beauty, with a mop of silvery-blond curls, standing on the cart-tail, putting on a sleeveless coat of scarlet velvet.

'Scarlet devil!' shrieked the priest, pointing at Gabriel. 'Why do you exploit the misery of the poor and the sick, you demon?'

'Where's this reward you mentioned?' said Garvey blithely.

'Your reward's awaiting you in the Fiery Pit!'

51

fumed the priest, running on the spot and punching the air with fury. Garvey toppled him backwards into the lock-up and bolted shut the door again.

As they continued their journey out of town, Gabriel sat very quiet beside the playmaster. 'What does "exploit" mean?' he asked at last.

Without the least hesitation, Garvey replied, 'To help and succour, lad. That priest didn't like you helping the poor and sick.'

'Ah!' Gabriel nodded, but he did not really understand. His mother had brought him up to hold priests in fearful reverence. He looked back and listened to the pounding on the door, until the lock-up was out of sight. Why should anyone mind a person working miracles? What with cursing priests and so very many sick people, the world suddenly seemed an unkind, unhappy place. So much work for one angel. Gabriel felt weary.

As they rolled on to the pound meadowland, Gabriel climbed down inside the cart so as to stay hidden until the right dramatic moment. Garvey would never let him be seen by strangers before the atmosphere was right. From inside the belly of the cart, peering through knotholes in the wood, he could see and hear the acres of people from Pontydd. They were speaking a foreign language, or so it sounded to him—quite different from the priest's—and many were groaning pitifully, or struggling painfully to get to their feet. Some were in hairy shirts and bare feet. A paltry little band struck up a welcoming tune, and children threw flowers awkwardly overarm. What looked like a whole detachment of maimed soldiers was sitting under a tree playing cards. An old woman, kneeling on calloused knees amid the buttercups, interrupted her prayers to shoulder away a cow grazing its way across the meadow. Twelve hares were roasting on forked twigs over a charcoal fire.

'It's like a fair. All these people enjoying themselves,' thought Gabriel, as he climbed the ladder (concealed now between the double thickness of the backdrop) to his throne behind the hinged clouds. 'And all because of me.'

Then Garvey cancelled the performance. The Lord of the Manor had sent word that he wished to see the players. Leaving behind the property wagons, and giving Lucie instructions to collect tributes from the people of Pontydd, he drove the pageant up to the Hall.

The Lord Llewellyn had expected them to act inside, but there was no way in which the pageant could be brought in through the doors. Gabriel was sorry. He longed to see the majestic height of a nobleman's banquet hall and to eat swan stuffed with capons and quail as his mother had told him the gentry did. But Garvey insisted on an outdoor performance. 'You wait, lad. Afterwards he'll offer us all houses and pensions, and take us up to London to show us to the King.'

The opening music was greeted by a torrential shower of rain that drummed with deafening force on the stage and put out the fires of Hell. Gabriel, sitting under a narrow sort of canopy built to protect his wings, had his lap full within minutes. The Lord Llewellyn, sitting beneath a brocade canopy and eating a bowl of figs, eyed the pageant with a mixture of amusement and contempt. There was nothing in his chinless face of the awesome wonder that Gabriel usually looked down on. There was just a kind of suspicious boredom.

When it came time to fling himself into the cradle of the flying harness, the back scenery was slippery with rain, and Gabriel's bare feet slithered against the paint so that he plunged nose down, the harness slipped down to his hips, and he sawed to and fro, arms outstretched.

'Fetch me my long bow,' jeered the Lord Lle-

wellyn, 'and I'll shoot me that winter goose up there.'
He threw a fig at the flying angel which Gabriel was
quick witted enough to catch one-handed. It was the
only part of the performance which won applause.

At the end, the nobleman called them charlatans
and beggars and told them that if they were his, he
would have them all flogged and their noses cut off.

Even after the fire, Garvey had never looked so
wretched. Gabriel's heart went out to the playmaster.
Unable to pour out any abuse on such an august
gentleman of the realm, Garvey could only bow
respectfully and struggle to turn the pageant in the
small yard of the mansion. 'Back to the glebe,' he
muttered. 'We can fit in a show before nightfall.'

The sun came out. The wet costumes began to
steam. In his sodden, crushed red velvet, Gabriel felt
like a flayed mole. And when they got back to the
meadow, Lucie had sent all the people home, refusing
every one of their eager tributes. The day was a wash-
out.

Everything was redeemed by the touch of his duckdown quilt. Wrapped inside it, Gabriel listened to yet
more rain drumming on the stage overhead, and knew
he was safe, however hard the wind blew or the rain
rained.

Garvey was not in his bed. He was arguing with
Lucie about the lost tributes of Pontydd. Gabriel
watched them through the knothole beside his pillow,
their gaberdines stretched out above their jerking
heads, like two long-legged birds pecking at each
other in the rain. He watched until his eyes began to
feel heavy and he was ready to sleep.

'Gabriel. Psst!' It was Izzie. She came crawling
across the pitch-black floor, the scuff of her knees
completely muffled by the clatter of raindrops.

'Uh? What? Oh, it's you.'

She felt her way towards his voice, her hands trying to make sense of his feet in the darkness. Then she found his hand and followed his arm up to his face. Her hands were cold and wet with rain, her eyes less well adjusted to the darkness than his.

'Hello,' she whispered. 'I've missed talking to you. Father and I have missed talking to you. Garvey forbad us. Are you comfortable in here?'

'Yes, very, thank you.'

'You're not afraid of the dark?'

'No! It's wonderful. It's warm. Feel my quilt. Have you got one like this?'

'Not exactly.'

'It's better even than when I was home—all my brothers and sisters in bed with me. This is more peaceful.'

'But you want to go home one day, don't you, Gabriel?'

'Oh yes!'

'. . . Shshsh! . . .'

'Oh yes,' he whispered. 'One day we'll ride into a town where my mother and father are in the audience, and they'll see me . . .' And he explained about the Wishing Game. 'When I find them, maybe I'll stop. Do you think I ought to stop? Or should I go on till I die?'

'Oh, I think your mother must miss you terribly,' said Izzie, and her voice was very earnest. 'Everyone ought to go home if they've got a home to go to. Father and I, we haven't got anything except the plays. Father put everything into saving the plays. We've nowhere to go, and Garvey keeps the purse. He won't . . .'

Gabriel did not like the subject of Lucie, or the criticism of Garvey he guessed was coming. So he said quickly, 'Do you ever wish for anything, Izzie?'

She was a long time in answering. 'Only to be a boy. Only to wish that I'd been born a boy.'

'Oh why?'

'. . . Shshsh . . . To save the Words, of course. The words of the plays. They were passed down father-to-son from Father's great-great-grandfather to him, and every one of them acted on the pageants, father and son. Now the plays are dying and Father's got the memory of them locked up in his head and no one to pass them to. No son, you see. Only me. Girls can't play on the pageants. Girls can't play any kind of play. Of course I wish I was a boy. Don't you see how sick he is? I did that. I broke his heart, I'm sure.'

Something warm and wet dropped on Gabriel's forehead which was not a leak in the staging: Izzie was crying bitterly. 'Oh Gabriel, you've got to do something. You've got to put a stop to this. Garvey's twisted his dreams and taken the pageant from him and turned the plays to his own ends and made him a party to this . . . this *blasphemy*! Father would leave, but he stays on and stays on out of fear of what will happen to you. I made him. I made him promise. Gabriel, you must put a stop to it. It's like a nightmare now. Garvey's sold our souls into damnation. You saw that priest! You saw what Garvey did to him! Pretty soon they'll send constables after us for doing such things! Run away before they come. He was born for a hanging, that one. That Garvey.'

'But that priest deserved it! He didn't want me to help the sick and sorry!'

'Oh you ninny!' She slapped at him in the dark. 'Do you still not understand? You don't work any miracles. There *are* no miracles!'

'I've seen them! I've seen eighty-three at least!'

'. . . Shshsh . . . They were Garvey's doing. Garvey fixes them—like he did that first time in Horsey, when he paid that waster to act blind.'

'But he *was* blind!'

'Keep your voice down. He was no more blind than you or I. Didn't you recognize him for that man we

56

gave a ride to on the road? Garvey planned it with him then. In every second town we reach, he finds some villain or slut to act up in the crowd. He hardly needs to do it now, though. So much miracle-madness. People are so trusting and hopeful, they only have to see you to imagine they're cured. Cured? It'll last till tomorrow. Then they'll find we've taken their money and their presents and left them their pain. An angel! I never believed so many people could be so stupid.'

'Well, go away, then!' said Gabriel loudly. 'You're lying. Go away. I trust the Master. He's kind to me. He gave me a quilt and peacock wings and a velvet coat . . .'

There was a kind of angry sob in the darkness. 'Now I believe what the countrywomen say about peacocks—they won't have a feather in the house— the Evil Eye they say it brings.' Her hands wrung at his wrist. 'For *me*, Gabriel. Tell Garvey no more miracles, for *my* sake.'

'I understand.' Gabriel understood. The Devil hates miracles. The Devil tempts all God's creatures so as to keep goodness out of the world. So this was the Angel Gabriel's temptation: to stop working miracles and run away, because Izzie begged him to, and cried in the dark. He clenched shut his eyes so as not to see the pale oval of her face through the shadows. And he thought very hard about that broken web of England and the busy spider mending it strand by strand. 'I *AM* an angel,' he sobbed out loud. 'I'm sorry, Izzie. I know you can't help not believing. I'm so sorry you're the devil-man's daughter. It's not fair on you.'

'The devil-man?' When he opened his eyes, he could see her face quite clearly, it was so close to his. Her black eyes were frighteningly ringed with white. 'Is that what you think? Because he plays Lucifer? You stupid, silly, idiotic baby! You poor darling boy! What does that make Garvey? God? Ha ha! That's priceless. Oh Gabriel, Gabriel, you've got it completely the wrong way rou . . .'

The trapdoor in the base of the cart dropped away and revealed a square of sickly grass lit by watery moonlight. Garvey's head appeared. He climbed the ladder, holding up a cord taken from the throat of Hell which gave off a red light as it smouldered. He said, 'I heard something. That girl's in here, isn't she? I heard her say your name.'

Gabriel did not speak. He knew that Garvey's eyes could see nothing, coming in from the relative lightness outdoors. The boy could feel Izzie's body brush past him as she crawled into a corner. If she could make her way along to the right ladder, she would be able to climb up to the painted clouds high overhead. He would pretend to be asleep.

'It's no good, girl. I heard your voice in here. Didn't I tell you to keep your evil-wagging tongue away from the boy? Didn't I tell you what would happen if you tried to turn his thinking?' But Garvey had his back to Izzie and it seemed she might escape unseen, as she set one foot on the bottom rung of the ladder to Heaven.

The burning cord whirled round in Garvey's hand. A red glow spread out across the floor almost like blood, and washed against the back wall. One white foot was just visible still, below the backdrop. He reached out and dislodged it from the ladder rung, so that Izzie slipped downwards into his arms.

Gabriel threw back his quilt and knelt up. 'Please don't hurt her, sir! She didn't do anything!'

Garvey's voice came back warm and reassuring through the gloom, above Izzie's struggling. 'I wasn't going to hurt her, son. Just tell me what she said to you. I thought you were asleep.'

'She doesn't think I'm an angel, that's all. It's all right. I don't mind.'

Garvey was holding Izzie out over the lower

trapdoor, one arm round her waist and the other across her throat. 'But you didn't *believe* her, did you Gabriel?'

'No, he didn't believe me,' said Izzie.

'No, I didn't believe her,' said Gabriel quickly.

'Well *that's* all right then.' And Garvey dropped Izzie down through the trapdoor. She fell with a sharp cry of surprise, and the ladder overbalanced on top of her.

Garvey came ducking across the compartment and sat down beside Gabriel, tucking the quilt round him. 'You won't be troubled by those French vermin again,' he said soothingly. '*Monsieur* Lucier and his brat are leaving our happy little family. What do I need them for when I've got my little Angel Gabriel, eh?'

'Lucier? Is that his real name?'

Garvey laughed. 'French scum,' was all he said.

'That's why he's called Lucie,' said Gabriel, almost to himself.

'Forget him. I don't want to hear that man's name ever again, world without end. Amen. Got it? Not from now till Doomsday. Son.'

CHAPTER SIX

PLUCKING ANGELS

GABRIEL CLIMBED up to his perch, and examined his face long and hard in the silvery mirror. Then he turned and surveyed the camp spread out below him. Coils of steam writhed off the wet grass under the early heat of the sun. Nearby, Garvey was fastening his boots and Adam of Rochester and Jack of Longleigh were feeding the horses. At a distance, the figures of Lucier and Izzie stood like souls in purgatory, chest-deep in the seething vapour. They were watching the camp pack away for the last time before it moved on without them. The pageant, covered with sunlit waterdrops, looked like a glittering vision floating on cloud.

'I wish them to stay,' said Gabriel grandly, standing up and spreading his arms wide in pointing at the Luciers.

Garvey chortled and went on fastening his boots.

'Do you hear me, playmaster? I wish them to stay!'

Garvey straightened up. 'Who's feeling grand this morning? Don't you fret, child. We're better off without them. You've too much softness in you.'

Gabriel hesitated and bit his lip. Then he breathed in deeply and said, '*I'm* the angel. *I* decide who stays and who goes!'

Garvey opened wide his bright blue eyes, strained wide his long, dark lashes. He was on the grass and Gabriel was on the wagon. The playmaster had to walk all the way down to the end ladder before he could climb up on to the stage. As he came, he blustered and snorted and black veins stood out in his forehead. Gabriel sat down again, squirming, his grand voice shrivelling to a whimper. '. . . in fact I'm thinking of going myself!'

'What's that? What did I hear? Here's me thinking I woke me and dressed me this morning, and all the time I'm still in bed and dreaming. I dreamed I saw a boy giving himself airs—preening himself like the Queen of Sheba. I thought I heard a thankless boy raising his voice against those that clothed him and suckled him and spent out a fortune on the making of him. Thanklessness is a terrible thing. It turned Lucifer's skin into black scales and plucked off his wings. God hates it above all things. Oh how He hates it! Almost as much as I do! It's a foul thing in a boy. A thousand leeches can't suck it out of him. Only a beating can shake it from him!' He came up the steep Hill of Heaven on all-fours, his boots scuffing the flowers out of their holes and his fingers scrabbling.

'I didn't mean it! I didn't mean it! I was joking!' howled Gabriel.

'I *MADE YOU!*'

'I know! I know you did, Master!'

Garvey's head reached a level with Gabriel's feet, knees, head. The silver halo dazzled his eyes and he almost lost his grip. As he teetered on the narrow platform, with peacock feathers moulting in his fists, Garvey wrenched the mirror off the scenery and threw it down on to the stage. Dented, it rolled round and round on its rim with a loud, tinny noise before clattering flat. 'Funny joke,' said Garvey, clutching his angel by the shirt.

'I'm sorry. I'm sorry. I'm sorry,' whispered Gabriel. 'I wasn't being soft. It's just that . . . It's just . . . Luci . . . the French vermin might make trouble for us, I thought—stir up the countryside against us!'

Garvey was startled. '*You* thought that? All by yourself? I thought you liked the girl . . .'

'Who? Me, sir? No, sir!'

'Did she say that's what they'd do? Is that what she was saying to you last night? Was she?'

'No! But they're both in league with the Devil, I'm sure of it. Angels know that sort of thing. Sir, we ought to have them nearby us, where we can see what they're up to . . . where they can't betray us without destroying themselves as well. Me, like Izzie? How could you think it? She says I'm not an angel. I hate her. Just because she cooks well and grooms the horses and mends the props and . . . And who could you ever get to play Satan so wicked? He's wickeder than any!'

Garvey picked thoughtfully at the peacock wings above Gabriel's head. 'And you thought all that out by yourself, did you? You could be right, son. You could be right. And who am I to argue with my Angel Gabriel, eh? Eh? Ha ha!' He stepped over Gabriel's knees and clambered down the ladder, mumbling. At the bottom, he paused and looked up, smiling one of his best smiles. 'Did you say you were thinking of leaving, did you?'

'No, no. Not really. I was just joking, Master.'

'Funny joke. Well, if ever you think of leaving, you just come and talk to me about it. I'd have to make arrangements, you see. I need a bit of time—warning, you see?'

'Yes, sir. Thank you, sir.'

'That's what upset me, see? The thought of losing my boy.'

'I see. Thank you, Master.'

So Izzie and Lucie were told they would stay. Not invited, but told, and basted roundly with curses and abuse by the playmaster. To Gabriel's surprise, they agreed to come back. They bowed their heads meekly in the face of Garvey's insults, and accepted that they

62

would receive only their board and keep. It was as if Lucie's pride had been purged away by standing in that vat of swirling morning mist. He did not complain when he found that his sleeping place had been claimed by another player; nor when Garvey told him to wash the mud off the wagon wheelrims, and forbad him or Izzie ever to speak a word to Gabriel. That afternoon, they performed the *Fall of Lucifer*, but it was not with Lucie. He said, 'The words have gone out of my mind.'

The audience could not have told it apart from *Christmas* or the *Assumption of the Virgin Mary*. They watched none of it. Their eyes were on the Miracle-Worker, the Angel Gabriel, perched in motionless splendour on a silver-gilded cloud, his hair awash with sunlight and his magical face worn like a mask that concealed some greater magic. Once in a while he spoke, in a pure and reedlike voice that escaped like smoke above the pageant, and was audible to hardly a one.

Behind his blank face, Gabriel was playing the Wishing Game. He was irritated when a cue to speak interrupted his imagining. Still, two verses only, and not another word to say. He let his eye run slowly along the faces in the audience.

It was no longer a strange sight to see blind men at a spectacle. They were commonplace. So were one-legged soldiers, women bent double with rheumatism, gouty noses, coughing children, broken arms, wasted goats and winded horses. The smell of evil embrocation drifted up even as high as the clouds of Heaven. The healthy stayed away, or hovered sceptically at the back of the crowd, talking as they waited for the first miracle. Gabriel looked for his parents—even though he knew by the local accents that he was far, far away from his own countryside. It was a part of the Game: it could not be skimped.

Suddenly his eye fell on one stubble-shaved neck

and back of head. His heart cannoned round his chest like a bullock in a pen. The head turned. He knew the ear and the wisp of eyebrow that bushed out beyond. The face turned, and the Angel Gabriel's shoulders began to drop forwards, his chest to contract, his elbows (which had struck such a heroic posture) to wilt inwards. The eyes in the face expressed no surprise when they met with Gabriel's, and winked. The Mason had long since spotted his apprentice perched high up in Heaven.

Colley the Mason came blundering through the crowds, treading on the sick laid out in rows on the ground. He pushed aside a woman kneeling on the stony ground. His swinging pack of tools knocked over little children as if they were skittles. Gabriel was spellbound, transfixed.

The Mason climbed the spokes of the cart wheel, grunted with the exertion of climbing over the rim of the stage, and rose to his feet where the golden pavilion hid him from Gabriel's view. The boy looked around wildly for Garvey, and saw him leaning against the property wagon quietly chewing sugar-beet. God's perch was occupied by a different player who was slumped in his throne half-asleep, an ale mug between his feet.

The droning verses down below petered out. The audience stirred restlessly.

'Listen to me, brethren! Bear witness to me!' The Mason's voice rasped over their heads like the rip-saw he used to cut stone. 'For ten years I was a mason, carving ornaments for God's holy churches—offering up the fruits of my labour to Him in Heaven who carved Man from Eden's clay! But three years ago—oh blackest day, I can't even now bring myself to speak of it—a fall, an injury. For three years now, I've carried this pack with me from place to place—a penance, a mortification, a burden that weighed as heavy as sin—thinking never again to open it, never again to be asked to take out my chisel or swing my mallet. I ask you? What good is a mason whose arm—mark this!—whose arm is shrivelled to nothing—as thin as a chicken's neck it was—as weak as the dribble from a baby's chin. That's how I was, people, and look at me now!'

He paced in and out of Gabriel's view, rolling back the sleeve of his dust-grimy shirt and baring his hairy left arm. 'One sight of this boy here—this gift from God—and I felt all at once a burning in my arm. The muscles swelled and twisted as if some snake was coiling itself around and about. The pain, oh, it was sweet—like a belly too full of beer. But see what my reward's been for those years spent glorifying God at my craft.' He stopped again by the pavilion and, with his eyes fixed on Gabriel and a demented grin on his pock-marked face, rent the golden cloth from bottom to top. Little flecks of gold whirled around him in the air, like motes in a sunbeam. 'I can only weep and wail that my years of workless wandering have left me no riches to offer this holy infant! Behold what I give! Behold how I lay down the great weight of sorrow I have carried with me so long. At the boy's feet! My mason's tools at the feet of the Angel Gabriel!'

The audience heaved upwards and broke like a wave, applauding, stamping, weeping, shouting, wailing with bitter envy and writhing to soak up a little of the surplus magic in the air. The company formed its well-rehearsed line in front of the pageant, their scarlet purses held out like gaping mouths. The Mason waded up and down among the crowds allowing the womenfolk to feel his arm and kiss his dirty hand as though it were a holy relic. Gabriel lost sight of him in the press.

Raising up the wooden clouds to hide himself from the public gaze, he hurried trembling down the ladder and hid in the dark cart, under his quilt.

At length he heard the horses being backed in

between the shafts, and felt the wagons jerk into motion. The baying of the crowds died away. The rap of coins falling on the staging overhead stopped. The trapdoor below the golden pavilion opened and a stifled beam of sunlight shone into the cart.

'Aren't you going to come out and greet an old friend?' called the Mason's voice.

CHAPTER SEVEN

BLACKMAIL

WHEN GABRIEL emerged, Garvey was just paying the Mason his fee for being 'cured' miraculously. He also handed him his bag of tools and said, 'You'll be wanting these, before you go.'

But the Mason pressed them back into Garvey's arms, grinning. 'Nay. I'll not be needing them. I made a gift of them to the lad, didn't I? I've changed my profession, after all.'

'You have?'

'I'm a Mystery actor now, friend Garvey—like my curly little apprentice . . . should I say, my little, *one-time* apprentice. Isn't that right, Gabriel?'

Garvey showed no surprise. He clearly did not expect to escape so easily. He could read the threat in the Mason's words, the blackmail; he wore a wry sort of a smile, and clapped the bully on the back. 'Welcome to the company, then. You can see we've made quite a saint out of your little Gabriel.'

The Mason nodded and made scooping gestures with his arms as if inviting Gabriel to give him a hug. 'I always knew you'd fare well, lad. Didn't I always say to you that you had your uses? Don't be shy, son. Come and shake my hand. We're in business together now!'

Gabriel shuffled forwards, crippled with terror. He held out his hand and the Mason crushed it inside his own until tears stood in the boy's eyes. 'Where's

Squit?' was all he could think of to say.

'Ah. Well. A sorry accident, that. Roof work. He fell.'

Gabriel had not cried out as the Mason squeezed his hand, but now he wanted to scream and drag on Garvey's sleeve and say, 'Make him go away!' He kept silent.

'As pretty as ever and just as dumb, I see. Well, you can fetch my partner and I a stoop of liquor, angel-face, while I warn him about you. He may not know what a lying, idle little slummock he's taken under his wing.' And as Gabriel walked away, the Mason was heard to say loudly, 'I hope you keep him tied up at night. He's a runner, you know.'

Just then, the day's takings were brought to Garvey by Davey of Carlisle. The Mason reached over and snatched the purse, emptying about half of the contents into his own hand. He looked up, wide-eyed, at Davey's gasp of disbelief. 'Just enough to buy myself a wagon, lumpkin. I'm not a greedy man. But I've got to have somewhere to lay my head down, don't I? I'm your new tally-man, didn't you know? Till I find a suitable wagon, I'll take the one on the end. Go and empty it out. Seems to be full of bed-rolls and clothes and dross.'

'Empty it yourself if you've got the gall!' said Davey in astonishment. One of the bed-rolls was his.

The Mason's hand shot out and caught hold of Davey's ear as if he would tear it off. 'And when I've done emptying, I could come back here and empty your brains on the ground, couldn't I?' As soon as he was released, Davey ran to the wagon, and the bed-rolls and personal property of the minor players flew out of the back of the Mason's new accommodation. 'Get rid of him,' said the Mason, watching Davey work. 'I don't like him.'

Gabriel ran straight to find Izzie. She was sitting beside her father who seemed to be asleep on his back in the grass. 'Izzie! Izzie! Where can I find liquor? They want liquor. I don't know where to find any! Please!'

She got up, glowering, without a word, and went to fetch the drink, leaving Gabriel staring down at Lucie. The devil-man opened his eyes and shielded them against the brightness of the sky. 'Don't fret yourself, child. He can't hurt you. He can't afford to. You're the treasure in his purse; he won't spill you.' Lucie's voice was low and soft, and his black eyes traced Gabriel's outline against the blue sky. 'He may make life unpleasant for the rest of us, but he won't smash the magic cup before he's drunk from it good and deep. He'll want things to go on just as before, while he helps himself to a share of the takings. The share will get bigger and bigger. Garvey will get madder and madder. But he won't be able to say no while the Mason holds your apprentice-bond. Blackmail. It's the strangling of one snake by another. We'll just stand by and watch, we three.'

Izzie returned with the cups of wine, saying softly to her father without looking at Gabriel, 'Wasn't I right the first time I saw this boy? I said he'd bring trouble to us all.'

Lucie did not raise his voice or his head. 'Hush, girl, and don't make a show of your ignorance. If it hadn't been Gabriel, it would have been some other angel along the way. Garvey's had this scheme in his mind as long as I can remember. And another boy might not have had the wits or the gentleness of this one.'

Gabriel crouched down, looking furtively over his shoulder. 'You understand! You won't let Garvey know, will you?'

Izzie tossed her head disdainfully. 'Understand? All I know is that *you* told Garvey we were in league with the Devil. And *you* persuaded Garvey to keep us on, unpaid, like prisoners, for fear we raised the country-side against you!'

Lucie plucked a stem of grass and chewed on it, smiling up at Gabriel with a conspiratorial wink. 'It was the only argument Garvey would listen to, wasn't it, lad?'

Gabriel nodded furiously and gabbled with relief: 'It was no good pleading with him. I tried commanding him—as if I were an angel—but he only got nasty. So I said the only thing he would believe. I couldn't let him leave you behind. Izzie's right: I did bring you all your trouble. But I had to make him keep you on. Izzie said you've nowhere else to go!'

Lucie laid his hand against Gabriel's cheek; it seemed to cost him effort to lift his arm, because a sweat broke out on his top lip. 'Best get back to the bearpit, eh son? And don't be afeared. I won't let anything happen to you. Not after what you did for us.'

Izzie came and gave the cups into Gabriel's hands and kissed him on the forehead. 'I'm sorry,' she said. 'I didn't realize.' Gabriel shook his head furiously, then hurried back to the Mason as fast as he could go without spilling the liquor. His cheeks were burning.

The Mason bought himself a nest of a wagon, and squirreled up coats and boxes, pots and pans, church silver, salt meat, the wax seals off the petitions, ale kegs and coins of the realm. Having discovered where Gabriel slept, he poked about in the hollow of the pageant cart, gathering up the tributes and luxuries that had found their way down into the dark. He left with the boy's quilt across his shoulder, swaggering like a Roman emperor.

One small comfort Gabriel took from this act of theft, this barbarous pillage: it would at least make Garvey feel sorry for him. They would be united in hatred for the blackmailing looter. They would be allies. Garvey would understand the need for an end to the miracles. That night Gabriel sat on the planking where his bed had been, and rehearsed brave, off-hand, modest responses to the playmaster's sympathy . . .

'*What, boy, and has he taken the very bed from under you—the very pillow from under your head?*'

'*It's all right, Master. It's a warm night.*'

'*No, no, lad! We can't have the Angel Gabriel sleeping on bare boards!*'

'*Really. I can wrap myself in a cloak or something.*'

'*You poor child! Here, you must have my quilt. This is truly the bitter end! Now I see the folly of my greed!*'

Garvey was so drunk when he got back to the pageant that he knocked over the ladder twice before opening the trapdoor. He crawled on his hands and knees to his quilt and slumped down on top of it, breathing heavily and filling the darkness with the reek of beer.

'He took my quilt!' wailed Gabriel, disturbing Garvey from the brink of sleep.

'Uh? What? Shut your noise. You came off light. Count yourself lucky. He could have had the hide off your back. He's told me what a deadweight you were to him. He owns you still.'

Gabriel crawled off into a corner and scrabbled together a nest made out of costumes and coils of rope, and curled up in the centre of that. For a long time he lay awake, feeling the vibration of Garvey's snores clear through the trembling planks. Then he crept across to beside the Master's head and squatted there, clutching his knees, waiting for the playmaster to sense his unhappiness and wake up. Garvey's mouth fell open and his tongue lolled. He was deep asleep. Gabriel reached out a hand, meaning to touch the man's shoulder: his fingers got caught up in Garvey's ear. He woke up with a curse and with flailing fists. 'Uh? Who's there? What is it? What d'you want? What you doing?'

'Excuse me. I'm sorry. Please, sir. Can I talk to you?'

'Can you what?'

'It's just that you said I should speak to you—give you warning—if ever I was thinking of leaving. Well, I just don't think I can stay now that man has arrived. He frightens me so much, you see. I couldn't possibly act. It couldn't possibly be the same, now he's come. And anyway, I ought to go and find my parents. If I could maybe take twenty shillings. They could re-apprentice me. Of course, I realize you need warning—to make arrangements . . .'

A hand feeling blindly for throat or arm or hair landed in the middle of Gabriel's face, and Garvey's fingers clung on like a starfish, pressing it out of shape. Afraid for his eyes, Gabriel froze, like a hare picked up by its ears.

'Listen, you half-pint of mashed swede. My friend the Mason and I have come to an agreement. He generously agrees to go halves on you. We split you down the middle. I own your soul. He owns your body. I'm God, see, world without end. You ought to know that by now. There's only one place you can go to get away from God. And where's that, eh, Gabriel? Eh?'

'Hell, sir!'

'Hell, sir. And I happen to know that my friend the Mason has the keep of *that* place. So why don't you just settle to knowing your place and doing your job, and just maybe I won't let him tear you in shreds the way he's aching to do? Yes, sir?'

'Yes, sir.'

'Thank you, sir?'

'Thank you, sir,' whispered Gabriel.

'Thank you, Sir God. Tell me, "thank you, Sir God"!'

'Thank you, Sir . . .' Gabriel, having both hands round the playmaster's wrist, managed to pull his face free of the spread of fingers. '*You're* not God. No more than I'm an angel!'

'Oh-ho! So when did you work that out? I suppose your Uncle Lucie put you wise. You ought to take care, talking to the Devil.'

Creeping backwards into the darkness made Gabriel braver, more reckless. 'He may play the Devil, but he's a better man than you are!' He wished his voice had not come out piping and shrill.

'Is that so? Is that so? Is that so?' Staggering to his feet, embroiled in a bewilderment of eiderdown, Garvey slurred, 'Well, you know what God did to Satan, don't you? He sunk him in everlasting fires. So why don't I just go down to that devil-Frenchman's wagon and see how he likes burning . . .'

The height of the staging above the bottom of the cart was only eight spans, and Garvey was nine spans tall. He cracked his head on the trapdoor beneath the golden pavilion and fell to the floor like a lopped tree.

In the morning, his friendship with the Mason was still as strong and his hatred towards Gabriel just as hot—but he could not quite recollect the reason. He was simply aware that Gabriel's allegiance had changed, that he spent all the spare time he could with Lucie and the girl, and that he no longer believed he was an angel. But Garvey did not care what Gabriel believed, so long as he conducted himself on stage like the Angel Gabriel.

And that was guaranteed. For on the day after his arrival, the Mason took Gabriel aside and explained. 'I've forgiven you the breaking of your bond, boy. But don't go counting on my mercifulness a second time. I know how to deal with runaway boys now. Ask Squit. No one gets away from me. And if a boy did . . . well, I've the knowledge here' (and he tapped his head) 'of where that boy comes from and where there's brothers and sisters a-plenty to take in his place and use as I used Squit and the others before him. Get me, *pretty boy*? Get me?'

Day by day, play by play, the Miracle Pageant grubbed up the wealth of every village, hamlet and town. Summer died under the weight of falling leaves, and autumn filled up the ruts in the road with rainwater, like blood filling fresh clawmarks. They played only in the morning, to put themselves six or eight hours away from a place by dark. And the Mason employed ruffians with staves to ring the camp at night and fend off the pilgrims who followed after the miraculous Gabriel.

The gold of summer faded off Gabriel's skin, grew down to the tips of his hair, and on days when the wind blew, he shivered at the top of his ladder like a flag at a mast-head, his long shirt billowing full of cold air.

The company began to talk of passing the winter in the south-west, of hiding the pageant in a barn somewhere and over-wintering on the money they had taken. The Mason insisted they go on. His wagon was incomplete: he wished for the floor cavity to be filled with coins before hibernating in his velvet-lined nest.

He seemed to find a fascination in watching Gabriel. Through each performance he would stand at the rear of the audience, his arms crossed and his head sunk down into his body as he peered intently at the stage. He never missed. Perhaps he was waiting for Gabriel to make a bolt for freedom, or to denounce his masters from the stage as murderers and charlatans. Or perhaps he could not understand why the boy, though pinned like the serpent in Saint Patrick's cleft stick with no chance of escape, grew more and more cheerful each day. There was no denying it: Gabriel was happy.

74

After the performance, while the pageant was swilling its way through mud, finding out the boulders that had sunk deep into the roadways, Gabriel would sit with Lucie and Izzie in the smallest wagon of all, the kitchen wagon. Out of costume, he wore Lucie's cut-down clothes, and would watch for hours the barons of raw meat swing and drip, swing and drip, over wood planks dyed permanently blood-red. On an incline, all the pots and canisters and the huge stew cauldron would slide down the wagon and crowd him into a corner. But he shoved them aside like inconsiderate pushers-in at a concert, and went on listening to Izzie playing her pipe or Lucie speaking the verses.

Lucie was teaching Gabriel the verses. From the *Creation of the World* to *Doomsday* itself, he spoke them over, and sometimes he would recite in French. He never said he was teaching, or asked Gabriel what he had learned at the end. But Gabriel knew he was being taught the verses.

The scowl did not lift off Izzie's face, however. She sat over her sewing, complaining that her eyes were getting old, and the yellow wax from the candle, skewered and hung up above their heads on a thread, dripped on the backs of her hands and made marks like the stains on old women's hands. All the while her father was reciting, her lips moved silently. Just occasionally, she caught sight of the cooking pots bustling down the wagon towards Gabriel and pinning him in a corner, and then she would laugh and heave them back to the top of the cart.

When Gabriel took to sleeping in the kitchen wagon, Garvey did not object. He drank nightly with the Mason in the treasure cave he called a wagon, and a kind of normality settled over the grinding wickedness of the Miracle Pageant and its never-ending circuit.

The cold began to wake Gabriel early. One morning a loose cord was flapping in the wind, cracking the canvas alongside his ear. He poked his nose outside to see if he could tie off the cord. It was a dreary, blustery morning, and silent birds were sitting in the trees with their heads bowed. The weather-vane on the pageant was spinning and squeaking; its ribbons were beginning to fade and fray and knot. A fox had been in the night and left footprints in the dew, right up to the kitchen wagon. Gabriel followed the even pattern of pawmarks as far as possible: they carried his eye up to a distant knoll crowned with trees and wounded with great white scars of bare chalk. The hillside had been quarried for a great many years.

The hair rose on the back of the boy's neck. It was like seeing the lock for which he had carried around the key, year after ignorant year.

'What's the matter. You're letting in a draught,' whispered Izzie, sitting down beside him in the tail of the wagon. She had been watching him for half an hour staring out at the view, motionless.

'Nothing.'

'You know this place, don't you?'

'I don't know. No. It's like somewhere . . . I've seen so much country.'

'But you think you lived in countryside like this,' she murmured.

'I know I did. But where? Somewhere else, I expect. It just looks the same. Forget it. What good is it? I couldn't leave, not if we drove past my gate. The Mason knows where I come from. He'd find my family and kill us.'

Izzie put an arm round him. 'Did it ever occur to you that he didn't murder that other apprentice—that he only said he did, to frighten you?'

Gabriel thought deeply about this, then said flatly, 'No. It never did. I believe him. Besides . . .' He looked over his shoulder at Lucier, whose sharp angular body pushed up through his blanket like a stretch of land tormented by earthquakes into a mountain range. 'If I left, I would miss some people.'

Izzie began to laugh one of her rare, dazzling laughs and immediately covered her face with her sleeve. Her hair was long now. It swirled and broke across her hand. 'We can't talk here,' she said. So she chivvied him out of the cart-end and walked him away from the camp through knee-length grass. It was so wet and cold that they might have been walking in the sea, but she did not seem to notice.

As they passed one of the Mason's guards, they startled him out of dozing, and he hastily got up, cursing them and telling them not to go out of sight. Clearly the Mason had given orders that the Angel Gabriel must not be allowed to slip away. The dew soaked upwards from the hems of their shifts. Gabriel was torn between a longing to be back under his blanket and a passionate pride that Izzie was about to confide in him. He found he was walking as a dog walks, its head twisted round to gaze into its master's face, waiting for a stick to be thrown, wagging its tail.

But Izzie's black eyes never left the scarred, distant hillsides. She did not even look to pick her way round thistles in the long grass. 'He's counting on you, of course,' she said, and now that she was no longer whispering, her voice was slightly sharp.

'Your father?'

'He's put all his hopes in you. You're the son he never had.'

'*Who, me?*'

She frowned irritably. 'He's teaching you the verses, isn't he?'

'I don't know a half of them—not a quarter!' said Gabriel in a foolish panic.

'I do.' She said it quickly and with venom. 'I do.'

Gabriel stopped in his sodden tracks, overwhelmed with guilt. He felt like Jacob in the Bible, who stole his brother's birthright. Had he stolen Lucie's love away from Izzie? Just by being a boy?

Izzie did not wait for him. She went on walking, and he had to run and catch up when she began speaking again. 'But you have to go home. It's not fair for him to expect you to stay—especially now Garvey's made criminals of us all. You go. If you recognize your own area, you go. The Mason won't come after you. He'll be too busy finding another boy to play Gabriel. Anyone would do. Most boys would sell their souls for the chance.'

'Yes,' said Gabriel, though he felt as crushed as the thistle she had just stood on. 'Yes, anyone would do ... But what about the words? Don't they matter?'

She was walking so fast now, circling the camp, that he had to jog along to keep up.

'Matter?' She glared at him—one short, singeing glare of her black eyes, and her hair swinging round the jerk of her head. 'Of course they matter! How dare you! But teaching you isn't the only way! Father's a sick man. He doesn't think beyond tomorrow. He doesn't think ahead. No. If you spot a place you know, or hear the name of a town that's familiar, you tell me—no one else, mind—not a breath of a word to Garvey or my father—and I'll sneak you out ...' She broke off. 'I'm fourteen, Gabriel! I may not be a boy, but I'm *fourteen*!' And she suddenly turned back in the direction they had come and ran all the way, her wet shift slapping against her bare legs.

Gabriel took himself to the top of a steep grass slope and, lying full length in the grass, rolled from top to bottom, over and over and over, until he was soaking wet and extremely dizzy. It had been fun once, when he was little. He did not care much for fun just now. He wanted to empty his head of everything Izzie had said. But her words tumbled down the hill with him: '... the son he never had ... have to go home ... Anyone would do ... You go ... teaching you the verses, isn't he? . . . a sick man . . . I'll sneak you out . . . You go . . . You go . . . You go.'

'Maybe I don't *want* to go!' said the air jarred out of Gabriel's lungs as he rolled down and down and down.

An unnerving thing happened that day which made up their minds to over-winter. They set up the pageant in a village street, and not one cottager came out to greet them. Had they succeeded for the first time in outstripping the rumours of their coming? Would it be necessary to work the mock-miracle trick again during the show? Had this village really not heard tell of the miracle-working Gabriel? Their busy preparations got slower and slower and finally halted as the realization dawned that the village was deserted, utterly deserted. Not a soul remained in the cottages, inn, barns, stables.

'Nothing but ghosts here,' said the Mason in disgust. 'And ghosts don't pay.'

'They don't prattle, either,' said Garvey, slipping out of God's robe. 'We'll stay here.'

There was a general murmur of enthusiasm from the assembled company who dispersed in all directions, pelting down the alleyways and pushing down doors to find the best houses for themselves. The Mason, who had been going to protest, saw that his own strong-arm ruffians were among them, and knew that to argue would be to risk public defeat. So he wisely avoided a clash of horns in front of the herd. 'I'd been thinking of it,' he said. 'I've been travelling ten years now. It's time to try my hand at the settled life. Winter should give me a taste of it. All that wagon needs for an over-wintering is a little wife to warm it.'

There was no one much remaining to hear this— only Garvey, Lucie unbridling the horses, and Izzie and Gabriel standing by. 'You. You there. You horse-eating Frenchman. Lucifer. You'll oblige me and fetch a priest here who can do the marrying, and a skinful of wine for everyone and food for a month or more, since we're settling. I'll send one of my men with you, to see you don't run off.'

Lucie was all set to ignore the command—to go on doing what he was doing. But Izzie took the tack out of his hands, 'Go on, father. Do as he says.'

'Oh yes? And what do I use for money?' said Lucie peevishly.

'Use your own,' replied the Mason with a shrug. 'Isn't that the way of it? For the bride's father to furnish the feast?'

CHAPTER EIGHT

A STRANGER AT THE WEDDING

'ISN'T THAT right, bride?'

Izzie raised her eyes from the ground and looked, long and silent, at her father, then replied to the Mason, 'He has no money. Garvey took it all.'

'Aaah. Shame,' he jeered. 'Then Garvey had best pay. Nah. We'll take up a general collection. Everyone'll want to favour us with a well-wishing. The "little girl" there can gather it in: he's good at that.'

Lucie turned waspishly on his daughter: 'Don't just stand there. Go to the wagon till I tell you. I'll straighten out his thinking. Blood and sweat he can force from us, but there's an end.' Then he laughed over his shoulder at the Mason. 'You'll get no joy of this one. She's not for marrying, this one.'

Izzie took hold of her father's hands and spoke in a soft, monotonous sing-song. 'Yes he will, Father. I'm fourteen years of age. It's high time I was marrying. Mason Colley is a wealthy man with two trades. When else shall I meet such a man, given my situation? Mason Colley has been . . . *approaching* me these six weeks, and now I'm settled in my own mind, I can't think you'll stand in the way?'

The look on the devil-man's face was a foolish, exaggerated astonishment, like the face he wore when Lucifer was cast down from Heaven to Hell against all his expectations. 'You choose to marry this rank *cabbage*? This walking midden? Have I raised you like

81

a cow, for the slaughter? I forbid it. I don't give my permission. That's an end. I've said my say. Go to the cart.'

'Father. Think again,' said Izzie peaceably. 'I've set my face towards it, and it's for the best. You know Mason Colley has a powerful hold over us all. Don't anger him out of silly pride.'

She tried to embrace him, but he seized her by the arms and shook her till her teeth chattered. 'Do it then, you Magdalene! What? For the sake of a morsel of warmth and finery, you'd take him, would you? The richest man in the camp and no matter that his soul's too dirty for a horse to tread in. No better than a whore. I've done with you. Never speak a word to me more!'

His abuse beat in her face like rain so heavy that it forced shut her eyes. But when he paused for breath, her face was still implacable. 'Please, Father. Calm yourself. Don't make yourself ill. Once you give the matter some thought, you'll see the fitness of it. And you still have Gabriel!'

'And a better son he is to me than you've ever been a daughter!' raged Lucier, whereupon Gabriel sat down in the mud and wept silently, his head clamped between his knees to shut out all sights and sounds. The next he knew, Lucie was dragging him to his feet by his hair and hauling him impatiently towards the kitchen wagon. He muttered repeatedly. 'Let the Devil take her, then, and I'll dance on her face on Doomsday.'

Gabriel trailed behind whimpering, 'She won't will she? She won't? Say she won't!'

Astutely, the Mason sent another man to fetch the winter supplies and the wedding fare and the parson.

So that the pageant should not be seen by any outsider and news spread of where the Miracle-Worker had gone to earth, they rolled the various carts into two barns facing on to the street. Then they re-peopled the village, opening up the doors and window vents of all the cottages, and letting the moorland winds blow through, raising up spectres of dust and shrouds of dislodged spider's web.

Men who had been seasonal workers formerly began talking of going stone-gathering and ditching during the winter. But the Mason would not trust them to keep silent about the Miracle Pageant. He planned to keep them idle, like some ship's crew becalmed miles from shore.

The young men entered into the wedding, therefore, desperate for enjoyment, for fear they sicken of each other's company before spring. They started drinking before the parson ever arrived and, when he did, fell upon the beer kegs that came on the same cart as though they were men dying of thirst. The priest looked around at them and curled his lip. 'Let's be done and finished,' he said. 'Where's the husband?'

The Mason came down out of his cart wearing God's Creation robe because he had taken a fancy to its white ermine collar and the cabalistic sun, moon and stars embroidered front and back. He wagged his muddy boots, feeling uncertainly for each rung of the ladder: he had clearly been drinking already. Garvey, anxious to keep their line of work secret, met him at the foot of the ladder with whispered protests and badly disguised anger. Trying to take the cloak off Colley's back, he only succeeded in tearing it. The Mason cursed him roundly.

'And the wife?' said the parson unhappily.

Izzie had made herself a dress. It was neither bright, nor ornamented, nor ill-fitting, but she was such an unfamiliar sight out of boy's breeches and working boots and fustian shirt that the company burst out laughing, and barracked and whistled and cheered and blew kisses at her on her long walk from the cottage where she had been hiding herself.

An endless walk it seemed to Gabriel, watching

through the slatted door of the barn. Behind him, Lucie sat in the kitchen wagon. He had not moved for four, maybe five, hours.

'Won't you be needed?' Gabriel said. 'When my sister married . . .'

Lucie kicked the brake paddle which rattled noisily in its bracket. But at least the break in the silence seemed to break his trance. 'What did she say to you, Gabriel?'

'Say? When?'

'When you went off walking yesterday morning. Oh, I saw you. Did she say she was planning this?'

'No! she was . . . I can't tell you. It's secret. But it was about me, not her. She didn't say anything about her. She never does . . . except . . .'

'Except what?'

'Except the time she said she wished she were a boy . . . Oh do look! There she is! Why do they keep laughing? She looks so pretty!'

Lucie cursed, but dropped down from the cart seat and came to stand behind Gabriel, side-on to the door, snatching sidelong glances at the thing he did not want to see. 'There's something in it,' he groaned miserably. 'If I could just comprehend it.' Finally his eye was caught by the billowing of Izzie's blue dress, as the wind pressed it against her thin, flat-chested body. And he turned and gripped the struts of the gate, gazing out like a prisoner through the bars of his cell. 'The poor little mite!' he exclaimed, as he might had he seen another man's child being mistreated in the street.

A great urgency gripped Gabriel, who unlatched the gate and ran off round the barn to where the moor streamed towards him like downhill water. It looked a flat, unrelieved green—grass and moss and bloated, stunted bushes.

When he got back, Lucie was not in the barn; he could not see him anywhere. The riotous company

had pushed their way into the church, where demented birds, disturbed for the first time in who knows
how long, were battering themselves madly against the
rafters. Bird-lime rained down like sleet. The crowd-
ing pushed Izzie and the Mason further and further
forward until the parson had his back pressed against the
altar. He held up his hands as if loath that they should
come any closer and breathe on him. 'I doubt this
place is sacred,' he complained. 'Any Christian would
have cleaned out God's holy house!'

'Hold your peace, and get on,' said the Mason.
'Jesu, you've been paid enough.' The drunken din was
deafening. The priest was becoming genuinely panic
stricken. 'In nomine Dei dico tibi . . . You!' He
flapped one hand at the Mason. 'Your name.'

'Colley the Mason, son of Bartholomew of Sedgwick.'

'. . . Colin, son of Bartholomew of Sedgwick. And
you!' He snapped his fingers under Izzie's nose.

'Lizabette, daughter of Jean Lucier of Dover,' said
her father, shouldering his way through the crowd
and taking hold of her elbow as if to acknowledge
ownership.

'In nomine patri et filii et spiritu sancti, mulier et
homo estis. Now can I go?'

Izzie looked at her father and kept her eyes on him,
her head turned further and further over her shoulder,
as the Mason towed her away by her wrist through the
pushing crowd. It was over, and some were complaining that they had missed it. They barged after the
couple, towards the door. Someone was shouting,
'Do't again, Colley! Do't again!' At the church door,
Gabriel was waiting. He jabbed his arm out in front of
Izzie and there in his fist was a bunch of wet, fleshy
flowers—cow parsnip and vetch.

She took them with such sweetness, and grace, with
such a look of affectionate gratitude and pleasure, that
Gabriel felt like the Wise Man who presented

frankincense to the Virgin Mary. He was over-balanced and swept along by the company, across the bald greensward that encircled the church, and into the inn. The parson, too, was forced to follow, against his will. He leaned backwards, digging in his heels, yelping, 'Let me be! Let go of me! In God's merciful name, let me go my way!'

Rolande and Ydrys were told to strike up a circle-dance. Like a plucked daisy, it was a ragged sort of circle, and Rolande and Ydrys were resentful of having to play when they would sooner dance.

'Play your pipe, wife,' said the Mason, laughing inordinately at the novelty of having a wife. Izzie was all too glad to break free of the circle and run and fetch her pipe. Garvey stood her up on the beer-stained trestle where she stamped out the rhythm with one foot and played jigs on her pipe.

Gabriel sat on the table edge. Her father sat near the door, staring into a cup of ale which he did not drink. Swathes of rain cloaked the noisy inn like the bed-curtain drawn round a feverish and delirious child, while the dark, deserted houses of the rest of the village kept a silent, gloomy vigil round about.

The first time that the door opened and spilled yellow light out on to the dark afternoon street, it was the parson making a bid for freedom. He crammed on his hat, clutched up his cloak and ran. But when he reached the place where the cart had been, which had brought him twenty miles from the nearest town, it had been stabled out of sight. As he stood in the torrential rain, and peered this way and that, the Mason and Garvey stood with their arms round each other's shoulders, in the doorway of the inn, watching him in puzzled amusement.

'Stay till the morrow, why don't you?' said Garvey hospitably. 'There's plenty for everyone.'

'In this place? I'd sooner sleep in a used grave!' howled the parson.

'Why? What's wrong with the place?'

The man threw his hands this way and that, as if urging the cottages to speak for themselves. Gouts of rain tippled off his hat and blackened the black of his cloak. 'Don't you know a plague town when you see one? Every soul in this place was carried off this last springtime. All inside a month. A snail should keep to its own shell, that's what I say—not go crawling about the country creeping into another's. Gypsies and tinkers! Give me some transport for the love of God!'

He heard the tell-tale sound of a horse whinnying in the largest barn, and ran to unfasten the door. The gate swung outwards, and he found himself looking up at the massive head of a yawning dragon with creased cheek and jowl and a lolling red tongue. He gave a shriek that should have woken the village ghosts, and bolted down the road, shivering puddles into glittering clouds around him.

The dancers inside the inn were all fetched to the door by Garvey roaring with demented laughter, slapping his thighs and reeling in and out of the streaming rain. 'Look at him run! Just look at him scuttle!' Colley the Mason was not laughing.

For a few moments, Izzie kept piping, then allowed the recorder to drop from her lips and sat down beside Gabriel.

He said, 'Are you married now, Izzie?'

'I am, Gabriel.'

'And why's that, Izzie?'

'To get a son, Gabriel. To get my father a grandson before he dies, and to teach the boy the verses after.'

Gabriel took this in, nodded, then rested his head on her shoulder; she rested her head on his hair. 'You could always have married *me*, Izzie.'

'You're a bit young for getting sons, Gabriel,' she said, but at least she did not laugh. 'Besides, I can maybe make Colley be good to my father. Soon he'd have turned us off. Father is so unwise in his rages. Now he'll keep us on. There'll always be money—and food in father's platter, even now he's old.'

'Is he old, Izzie?'

'Old enough. He's past thirty. And he gets pains inside.'

This thought silenced them both until Gabriel said, 'Have you thought? You might get a daughter.'

'God would never be so unkind,' she said with determination.

The parson was out of sight. When the company came back inside, their mood was entirely changed. Izzie stood up, ready to play again, but they wanted no more dances. They were fretful and angry.

'Why do we have to go?'

'What's wrong with the place?'

'It's right made for us, ready and waiting.'

The Mason only snorted and cursed like a horse with croup. He could not bring himself to say the words, so great was his terror of plague. It was left for Garvey to explain how the village came to be deserted and why it no longer offered cosy prospects for a snug winter.

Some, like Lucie, were confident that Death had long since moved on out of the village. They wanted to stay. But there was no persuading the Mason. He was scraping the mud of the streets off his boots and dusting down his shoulders as if the rain itself might be contaminated.

'Where shall we go, then?' asked Gabriel.

Colley's eyes lighted on his former apprentice and his face gave that convulsive shudder, as of a man looking on something unendurably loathsome, before buckling into a grin. 'Well don't I know just the place we'll be made as welcome as Christmas! We'll go to *Gabriel*'s house! A play or two more on the way ... It can't be but fifty or eighty mile from here. I have the memory of it perfect in here,' and he stood with his hand spread on the top of his head, while the full implications sank into Gabriel's.

The company would settle like locusts on the household, demanding to be fed, sheltered, kept in ale and hidden from prying eyes. And faced with the fact that their son had not only absconded, breaking his apprentice's bond, but was earning his living by fraud—a bogus worker of miracles—his family would be forced to open their doors, obliged to beggar themselves in harbouring the Miracle Pageant right through the winter.

'You must go. At the very next place.' Izzie breathed the words so softly into Gabriel's ear that it was as if he had thought them himself. 'Without you to hand, he'll not trouble your people.' As Gabriel turned to look at her, her hair blew forward across her face in a blast of wind from the opening door.

'No!' Gabriel said.

'And I say yes,' said the Mason with malicious pleasure. 'What does my friend Garvey say?'

His friend Garvey was not about to reply. He had his finger up to his lips as a warning to Colley, but his eyes were on the stranger standing in the doorway.

Although he was completely sodden, with mud caking the hem of his cloak and doubling the size of his boots, there was a look of money and breeding about him. Wealth was in the weft of his streaming wool, and status in the bobbed cut of his clean, gleaming hair. This was a man of importance.

'Are you the men of the Miracle Pageant?' Expressions as blank as the bricks in a wall met the stranger's question. He made an irritable gesture of flapping his cloak to shake off the water. 'I found the pageant in the barn. You *are* the players. Do you truly work miracles?'

'No.' Garvey moved forward as if to defend his herd. The stranger might have a warrant for their arrest. But the man's obvious wealth was a temptation

Garvey could not resist. 'Though miracles sometimes occur while a certain companion of ours is close at hand.'

Gabriel had taken himself off under a table. The stranger peered between and beyond the silent, uneasy company, but he could not glimpse the boy. Even in better light, it would have been hard to make sense of the look on the stranger's face, torn between agitation and disgust. It was a thin, elegant face with bright spots of red on the cheeks, like a painted lady. There was a deep crease between his nose and the corners of his mouth, as if he was in the habit of sneering. 'Pah!' he said, with a small explosion of rain and spittle. 'I'd get no different answer, true or false. Well, to the Devil! I've come for you.' (For a foolish moment, Gabriel took him literally. Was this the Devil himself come to fetch them, black cloaked and wealthy, splenetic and anxious to be back in the warm place he came from . . . But Gabriel was in no position to speak up and say they did not want to go.) 'I've a place for you to bring your *ambulatory miracle-working*, your *itinerant saint*.'

The words were propelled at them like stones from a sling: a direct hit would have killed a bear. Their glancing blows stunned Garvey. 'We may not choose to come,' he blustered. 'Where is this place?'

'My fa . . . my mother's estates.' He flicked the corner of his cloak at Izzie to clear her off the table—as if to touch her would dirty his hands. Then he spilled himself a puddle of wine and, dipping one gloved finger in the puddle, drew a plan of his mother's estate-village in relation to the deserted plague village. A fly drowned itself in the puddle. 'Not above six miles,' he said.

'Across that moorland? In the wet? I regret, sir—it can't be done!'

'Tonight,' said the young man.

'In the dark? In this rain? Impossible!'

'You'll do it,' said the stranger. The candlelight shining directly up into his face threw his top lip, cheekbones and eyebrows into sharp relief, and blacked out his eyes. He reached inside his doublet and brought out a white velvet purse. 'You'll come. Here's half your fee now and the same to follow when you've done. If there's miracles, you'll get the same for each one. You'll come, all right. I'll lead the way . . .' At the door he turned and said in a clipped voice, 'Where's the Miracle-Worker? I want to see him.'

'He's at his prayers. I can't disturb him,' said Garvey unhesitatingly.

'But he's not dead yet?'

Garvey had to laugh. 'Bless you, sir. 'Course he's not dead or would I take this from you?' He was left standing with the purse raised in one hand towards an empty doorway.

The velvet purse was huge. Everyone could see that. It hung off all sides of his hand like a lump of uncooked dough. Quick as a thief, Garvey raised it to his collar and was about to drop it down the inside of his shirt when the Mason took a hold of his collar from behind and twisted it.

'You don't want to travel with that weighing you down,' said Colley. 'Let me carry it for you.'

'Half!' said Garvey sharply.

'All,' said the Mason, wrapping his arm across Garvey's throat. 'You wouldn't deny me—not on my wedding day. Or I might go telling that young man where you found your young Miracle-Worker. Eh? I'll maybe share the next one with you.' It was futile to struggle: the Mason was much stronger. He grasped the purse and thrust it inside his own shirt, under his armpit. 'Let's not delay the young squire. We've still to tackle up the horses and fetch out the wagons . . . Shift your roots, you toadstools! I'll be glad to get out of this plaguey hole. Where's my wife?

I'll take her in my wagon. That's where she belongs on her wedding night. Where is she? Who'll drive the bride and groom?'

But although she had been standing there just a moment before, there was no sign of Izzie. Under the table, she pressed her fingers against Gabriel's lips. Her black eyes were huge and rimmed with white. 'Please! He frightens me so much,' she whispered.

Two or three men, besides her father, had seen her creep under the bench. But such was the liking they felt for Colley the Mason that no one said a word. So he went to his wagon alone on his wedding night, and drove unaided up on to the moor, whipping his horses across the wilderness of black, tossing, wet grass. Gabriel watched him go, and prayed for the grass to roll over him and swallow him up, like the Red Sea engulfing the Egyptian charioteers as they chased the Children of Israel.

Izzie crept out last, and pinched dead the candle flame. She saw that its heat had completely dried up the wet streaks of the map drawn by the stranger's finger. Only the puddle and the drowned fly remained.

CHAPTER NINE

DOOMSDAY

MOST OF the night they followed the slouching figure of the young squire across the trackless moor. Now and then they lost sight of him below the skyline. Now and then there was lightning to point out the black holes, the crumbling trenches, the boulders scattered in their way like the droppings of some vast, vile dragon.

The driver of one wagon, carrying food and costumes, was alarmed by the dense dark shape of a monastic building welling up out of the horizon: he jerked his reins. The wagon smashed its wheel against a boulder and had to be abandoned.

'All those costumes! All that salt meat!' said Gabriel, looking back.

'After this we'll be living on quails and larks' tongues,' said Garvey, and he did not even turn round.

The pageant, though it rolled and wallowed, groaned and scraped its underbelly on the crests of every ridge, did not overturn or suffer any collision. Two men stumbled along ahead of the wheels treading out a safe path across the seething grass. They cursed and uttered muttered threats to desert, but on and on they walked until they made out a herd of wild cattle staring at them hostilely through the rain, and clambered aboard. The wheels soon graunched against a broken stone wall, and a worry of goats scattered like demons in the dark. The men once more jumped down from the wagon and found themselves ankle-deep in mud. But still the pageant rolled on towards its most highly paid performance of all.

By the time the towers of his parents' manor house appeared, the rider leading the way had begun to cough. They could hear it far ahead of them—a rasping, monotonous cough. He was a terrible rider. His feet hung clear of the stirrups, and he was arched over like a letter G in the saddle; his reins had slipped down round his horse's hoofs. Gabriel could sympathize: he too craved a night's sleep.

The manor house lay like a mother pig, suckling a huge litter of tiny huts and cottages, animal pens and cultivated strips of farm land. A strong wind chased the rain over their heads and away as they approached, and the trees tossing beside the walls made the outline of the huge house appear to tremble, as if it might roll over and crush all the homes of the people who depended on it. The house was moated on three sides, but the pageant rolled in across a narrow plank bridge and into a courtyard as spacious as any market square. The courtyard was overlooked by the lancet windows of the manorial home itself, and a large chapel. A party of saints danced colourless across a stained-glass window lit for a moment by lightning. Everywhere there was a reek of something acrid that made their eyes smart.

'Set up here,' said the young man.

'As soon as it's light,' said Garvey.

'Now,' said the young man. 'If the light's late in coming, you can play by torchlight.' And he stumbled away, hacking into his two hands.

'It's my guess his old mother's dying,' said Garvey in an undertone. 'That's why it's money-no-object for a miracle.'

The Mason looked uneasy. 'What do we do, then? What if she dies?'

'Then she won't be wanting her money back, will she? Nah—we'll give her something to make her feel like one of the Blessed, and ship her off to Heaven happy. The *Death of the Virgin Mary* would have done nicely. We must get a good Virgin again. Remind me in the Spring, Lucie. We've got no good Virgin. *Doomsday*, then. And Gabriel—Gabriel?'

'Yes, sir.'

'Gabriel, when it comes to escorting the good folk up to Heaven, you point straight at the old dame. Make like as if you're beckoning her. The rest of you! You're demons. Horse it up well and proper when you're gathering up the damned folk. Fetch in ten or twelve from the crowd and push 'em down Hell's Mouth.'

'They'll tear it with their damned boots,' complained Jack of Longleigh who had built the new Mouth of Hell. 'Can't we just seize on each other. Buskins don't do half the damage.'

'You've got all winter to mend it. Fetch in a dozen from the crowd and don't argue,' said Garvey tetchily. 'Children and old folk for the Blessed Ones. Not maidens. You can never tell with maidens these days. They're not so well behaved as they were formerly. Stir yourselves! There's all of Purgatory and Limbo to build. Yes. *Doomsday*. I like it. This place feels like Doomsday. Jesu! It even smells like Doomsday. What is that smell?' And he shivered energetically and swung his arms and clapped his shoulders. 'Jesu, I'm cold.'

Even when all the pageant was ready, it was still almost dark. They took no care to work quietly, hoping that someone they disturbed from sleep would fetch them out a hot drink or a bite of freshly-baked bread. Not a bit of it. There was not even a smell of bread baking—unusual in any village an hour before dawn.

A streak of white, like a slow-worm, stretched itself

95

along the horizon. It was soon hidden by a mush-rooming of peach and golden clouds, and at last the sun showed its rim like the rind of an orange. They changed into their costumes. Gabriel put on his white shirt and scarlet tabard with the gold embroidery. His hair, which now reached past his shoulder blades, curled as lustily as honeysuckle. As Gabriel took his seat at the top of the pageant, hidden by a wooden cloud, Garvey robed himself down below in the Mason's wedding robe, and Izzie emerged from nowhere to mend the tear in the shoulder-seam. The rising sun glared in the new, round, precious, shining, glass mirrors above Gabriel's throne and above God's, and filled the courtyard with a warm, flickering orange. A window hanging twitched in the manor house, but the only person to reappear in the yard was the young squire.

The spots of colour in his cheeks were much brighter than before, and he had a napkin crumpled in his hand; all that coughing had clearly started his nose bleeding.

'You don't think this is just for *him*, do you?' Izzie whispered to her father. But he did not answer. He was much paler himself, and looked a good deal sicker than the red-cheeked young man. The hard rim of Satan's hood exaggerated the gauntness of his face. 'Are you all right, Father? Shall I tell Garvey you're not fit?'

'No, girl. But I'll be glad when this is done with. That smell sits on my stomach.'

'What is it?'

'I don't know. Sulphur?'

The squire leaned against a buttress of the house, coughing and dabbing his nose. 'Begin then, why don't you?' he demanded hoarsely.

'Well, where is everybody?' retorted Garvey. The Mason looked out of his depth, confused. He too was feeling the cold, though it was a fair, clement morning.

'They'll come along. When you begin,' croaked the squire, sliding down the wall into a crouch.

The playmaster heaved an exaggerated sigh. The players melted away out of sight. The clouds rose up in front of God's throne. The pageant shook a little, and the weather-vane bobbed reverently, as Garvey climbed the concealed ladder, rung by rung, to his seat. A great silence, like the holding of a breath, stuffed up the sunny courtyard.

'When first I made this World right fair,
And madeth Man my likeness in,
I left him free to choose and dare
Whether he thrive or whether he sin.'

With no cushion of bodies to soak up the sound, Garvey's voice ricocheted off the house and chapel walls, and added an eerie aftermath to every sentence.

'But then I rued my deed full sore,
For everywhere did man and wife
Shrug off the keeping of my Law—
Shall such win everlasting life?'

Gabriel let the sing-song rise and fall of Garvey's voice lull him into a stillness, while his eyes travelled (for want of interesting faces) over the even rows of brick cladding the manor house, and the iron-outlined figures of the saints in the stained-glass chapel window. An angel hovered over their heads, blowing a yellow trumpet. The stern, slightly pained expressions on the saints' white and pink faces seemed to reflect fifty years or more of having a brass trumpet sounding in their ears. On the door of the manor house itself was painted—it showed now as the light brightened—a large, black cross . . .

'Sent I my Son to harrow Hell
And light the way for meek and mild
To climb the sharp and stony hill

To blessed Heaven's sunny peak . . .'

The young squire sitting against the buttress, keeled slowly over and sprawled face down on the pavers. At the same moment, a drumming and scraping of feet on the bridge over the moat signalled the arrival of the estate workers from the cottages outside the manor wall . . .

Garvey carried on:

'Soon will I quench the burning sun
That marketh out my day from night,
And by the light of blood-red moon
Will I my subjects sort aright.
Some up to Heaven, some down to Hell.
My doom I speak and change it never:
Some will I sink beneath my heel
And some shall I have with me for ever . . .'

They heaved like a single body rising up out of the earth, still covered in clinging soil; their arms round one anothers' shoulders, their hair matted to a uniform colour by sweat and filth, their clothes the same moth-eaten, slept-in brown, dangling straw from their beds. Some were carrying children, as though the tiny shapes were molten lead running out of their grasp and heavy past holding. They squeezed across the narrow bridge ten abreast—one hideous, brown, pestilential beast with a hundred buckling legs. Others came behind on hands and knees. Two wicker stretchers tossed on the beast's back, half spilling their shroud-covered loads.

The manor-house door had opened, and a woman in bare feet, with long grey hair hanging half-plaited over her shoulder, was moving towards the pageant like a magnet towards a lodestone. A bedspread of the most exquisite, intaglio velvet was clutched round her shoulders. It dragged down the steps.

The crowd jingled with all their wealth. Coins and

pots and pans and weapons and tools and horse tack jangled like a demented musical band, and each time someone fell, the clanging beast would sag, then lift the fallen back to their feet and sweep them on into the courtyard. Like ants over their nest they swarmed, black and confused. And their faces, their faces were above all beast-like. Every top lip was pulled back off the teeth, every eye was ringed round with a reddish bruising, while their cheeks cracked like tambourines as they cough, cough, coughed.

When they first moved far enough into the court-yard to glimpse Gabriel sitting on his cloud, the morning sunshine dazzled eyes that had been indoors for days on end. Then they loosed a universal cheer of sorts, perforated by coughing. They blessed him and called him their saviour. Then the pleas began—not unfamiliar to Gabriel the Miracle-Worker, but worse, much worse, so much, much worse.

'Heal me, highness!'

'Me first!'

'No, me!'

'My child, for the love of God. Not me but my boy here!'

When Gabriel turned in terror towards Garvey, the playmaster was already struggling to untangle his robe from the top of the ladder and to climb down. His mouth was a hard circle—as if he were howling, but silently. The look in his eye, when it met Gabriel's, frightened the boy more than ever—made his heart cower in the back of its cage. 'Keep them off me, boy! For Jesu's sake, keep them off me!'

Then Izzie was calling him from behind the pageant. 'Plague, Gabriel! *It's the Plague!*'

Up until then, the Mason, who had jumped from in front of the stage on to it, had jibbered indecisively and looked to Garvey for salvation. Now, hearing Izzie speak the lethal words, he opened his mouth and screamed shrilly, rending up the weather-vane and wielding it like a quarter-stave. 'Keep off! Keep off, you plague rats! Get off! Get away! Don't come near!' As their hands reached across the edge of the stage, he stamped at their fingers.

Gabriel stood up.

He spread his arms and he arched his back and he thrust his head as high into the sky as it would go. *'God's blessing on you! Stand still!'*

They did. The crowd stood still. Some fell down, forgotten by those who had been keeping them on their feet. The players froze, too, realizing that all escape from the yard was blocked by yet more plague-sufferers still on the bridge.

Remembering what Garvey had said about comforting the sick dame, Gabriel leapt to the end of the play and snatched at the only words that seemed the right ones for these poor corpses, these walking dead:

'Now take I up these Blessed Ones
Who lived full filled with truth and good.
Come Christians all. Through God's sweet son,
Are you ordained to dwell with God.'

They looked just like the Dead raised to life on Judgement Day, brought out of their graves and tombs, or cast up by the sea as it dried up utterly. The huge warped circle of the rising sun shone in their desperate faces and cast the shadow of the pageant over their lower bodies. Gabriel could see his own shadow, the shadow of his peacock wings, spreading out over them, and he felt the heat of the sun beat on his back. There he stood, a bogus angel standing between God the Creator and the people He had created, as they crumbled back into the clay they were made from. The sin of his blasphemy struck Gabriel like the sunbeams, between the shoulderblades, and pierced him to the soul. He knew what blow had knocked proud Lucifer, the first angel, out of the sky and hurtled him down to be the founder of Hell. It had been a spear of sunlight.

It seemed one hundred years that those poor people looked up at him—at Gabriel the fraud—and waited for a miracle. Then they began to glance about them with jealous, embittered eyes, wondering if someone other than they had been saved, whether God had favoured one and not another. Then an idea glimmered in one face—the idea of touching the Miracle-Worker—and instantly it was in every mind at once, with young and old alike fighting each other to be first up on the pageant.

One found the trapdoor in the base and, through it, the ladder to Gabriel's throne. The boy sat like King Canute who forbad the tide to rise and was forced to sit watching as it lapped higher and higher. The tide of plague rose up and up towards him. The same tide washed round Colley the Mason and swallowed him up. The faithful pushed past him, round him, and over him as if he were invisible, a stage property in their way.

'I'm sorry! I'm sorry! I'm sorry!' shouted Gabriel at the mob. He climbed away from their reaching hands, on to the very top of the gantry, breaking the spines of his peacock wings. Like Lucifer falling out of Heaven, he threw himself off the back of the pageant, not caring that the paving stones lay three leagues below.

He fell into the arms of the Devil.

Lucie, who had been calling to him all the while, unheard above the din, caught him in both arms and ran with him, up the steps and through the chapel door which Izzie was holding open. The whole company—all but for Colley the Mason—was ranged round the chapel when she banged shut the door and bolted it against the mob. Fists clamoured against it.

From inside, they heard the pageant rolled over on its back. They heard the tinny clatter of its properties rattled round the yard among running feet. The

Mason's voice shouted stronger than the rest, 'Let me in! The Devil curse you! Let me in!' But if they once opened the door, the plague mob would most certainly overwhelm them in searching out their angel, paid-for Miracle-Worker. And such was the liking the company felt for Colley the Mason that they put their fingers in their ears and turned away from the door, and stared straight ahead at the altar.

When Lucie put Gabriel down, he was blowing like a winded horse. With one hand he pushed the boy away from him, and with the other he tore off his horned hood and hauled at the tight collar of his scaly costume. His throat was wound round with flickering blue blood vessels, as though he was being strangled by asps.

'Father!' Izzie came running. But he held out the flat of his hand towards her. 'Keep away from me!'

'Why? What have I done? Father?'

But he just shook his head and backed away, and repeated over and over again, 'Stay away. Keep away from me. Both of you, keep away.'

'He's got it, don't you see?' called Adam of Rochester in a flat, unpitying voice.

Fists went on hammering on the door. Dozens and dozens of fists. 'Come out and save us! Angel Gabriel! Come out to us! Show yourself to us!' But they were weak fists. Between them, the Black Death and the Lung Plague had consumed the lord of their estate, his only son, and three-quarters of his estate-workers. And the Plague's teeth were sunk deep into the remaining members of the community. Soon the cluster of buildings would be as deserted as the plague village they had left on the moor's edge.

No one remained with strength enough to fetch a crowbar and lever open the flimsy chapel door— except perhaps the Mason, who was too bent on escaping the touch of the contaminated crowd. He fled and fled, and every door he found was painted with the black plague cross and every face he pleaded with was tinged with the red of plague fever. And a section of the crowd followed him everywhere, trying to persuade him to speak to the Angel—to intercede with the Miracle-Worker on their behalf.

Inside the chapel, only Izzie and Gabriel held hands. The rest of the company ranged themselves around the long, cold room, their backs to the wall, their eyes on the man opposite, their faces utterly inexpressive. They would not touch for fear—for abject terror that their former friends were carrying the seeds of death. Prayers sprang to the lips of men who had made a trade out of phoney miracles. Those who had long since forgotten their prayers, mouthed pieces of play, pieces of the Mysteries that had been recited like prayers for two hundred years.

Icier than them all, Garvey stood and trembled, as a rabbit trembles in every whisker and hair, staring at the altar, his lips spitting with the frenzy of silent recitation. He went for so long without blinking that his eyeballs dried. So when, at last, the lids rasped down, dry over dry, he uttered a short, horrified cry and put his hands up to his eyes, believing that, for his blasphemy, he was about to be blinded.

Lucier had taken himself up to the gallery of the chapel—a climb which cost him all the strength that was left him. From the other end of the chapel they could hear his breathing, hoarse and ruptured, even after it subsided into the rhythms of sleep.

'I must go and look after him,' said Izzie, disentangling her fingers from Gabriel's.

'He's got it, Izzie. Don't you go!' shouted Adam of Rochester from his lonely corner. 'Keep away from him, Izzie, or stay away from us till you're done for too.'

She paused with one foot on the ladder to the gallery. 'It doesn't matter,' she said.

Gabriel nodded and trailed after her. 'She's right. It doesn't matter.'

Someone shouted, 'Your wings won't save you now, lad!' But Gabriel trudged on up the ladder, knowing only that he preferred to be with Izzie and her father than alone in the chapel with these stony figures against its walls, all staring with stony eyes, and all too lonely to touch one another.

Lucie was sleeping an unnaturally deep sleep. Izzie sat at his head and Gabriel at his feet, while the sun moved gradually from shoulder to shoulder of the stained-glass saints in the window of the gallery, and cast a variety of colours across the scales of Lucie's costume. The effect was beautiful, as even a serpent is beautiful once the fear of it is overcome. Izzie played her pipe softly, breathily, while the sun shone through the stained-glass angel on to her face. It was long past noon when Gabriel suddenly burst into tears.

'Why Gabriel, whatever is the matter?' said Izzie brightly.

'*I'm not an angel*!' Gabriel raged, rocking his body to and fro.

Izzie leaned across her father to hold his hand. 'I thought you knew that, boy. I thought you worked that out long since.'

'I did! But in a sort of a way . . . oh, out there! Out there and in here! I want a miracle so much—I've wished for one so much. If I was one millionth part of an angel there *would* be a miracle. But I'm not. I'm nothing. I'm nobody.'

'Yes you are. You're Gabriel,' she replied in her reasonable, businesslike voice. 'No, you're not an angel, no more than any of us. But look at it my way: I never thought you were. I knew all along that you weren't. So if *I* like you, it can't be the angel I like. I must like the real Gabriel. Well, it stands to reason, doesn't it? My father here loves you like a son, so you must practically be my brother.' She was completely dry-eyed.

104

'But I can't do anything to help him!' Gabriel howled.

'So?' she said. 'You're here, aren't you?' And he noticed that she had stopped scowling. Or perhaps it was the white light shining through the milky angel that erased all the lines from her face.

Just then Lucie stirred between them. Puzzled, his eyes strayed along the line of saints, taking in each from head to foot until the sun shining through the last one dazzled him and his face wrinkled up. It went on wrinkling until Gabriel realized that he was laughing. Lucie reached out and grabbed his arm. 'I thought I was in Heaven, son! I thought I'd woken up in Heaven. It was that angel put me right. "My boy Gabriel's a better looking angel than that," I thought. By God, I'm as hungry as Elisha in the desert . . . Explain something to me, Gabriel.'

'What, sir?'

'When did you ever learn that verse from the end of the *Doomsday*. I never got so far in teaching you. It was for Garvey to speak it, anyway.'

Gabriel was confused: his memories were a jumble. 'I don't know. I can't remember. I just knew it.'

'A bit of a miracle, I call it,' said Lucie, drawing his long, thin legs up under him and getting to his feet. 'It gave us the time we needed to get in here.' He stripped off his scaly shirt and breeches and ran his hand over his armpits and groin.

'No plague, Father?' said Izzie.

'No plague, Daughter. Just the old trouble, I suppose. Just my plaguey heart betraying me. Are you feeling well yourself?'

'Very well. So is Gabriel. But we didn't all get inside, Father. My husband is still outside.'

For a fraction of a second, a strange, satanic glitter lit up Lucie's eyes and his fist clenched and he began to punch it in the air. Then his fingers unfolded and he crossed himself reverently and ducked his head. 'God forgive me for the thoughts I just thought.'

'Then God forgive me, too,' said Izzie, following his example. But her black eyes had the same satanic glitter in them as she climbed down the ladder from the gallery.

They found the various members of the company still rigid and separate, like a circle of tent pegs after the tent has blown away. Only one figure had subsided on to the ground, his face to the wall, and all their gazes were on him, terrified and arrow-sharp with hatred.

The three climbing down the ladder broke the spell that transfixed them, petrified them into plaster statues. 'He's brought it in here,' whispered one of the Mason's thugs. 'He's done for us all. Can't you smell the poison on him already?'

'No,' said Lucie sharply. 'No, I can't. Garvey! Garvey, what ails you, before these heathens beat you to death?'

The figure on the floor stirred and drew in its knees, curled up like an unborn baby. Garvey was crying. His voice, when he spoke, was muffled by his collar and unrecognizable—soft and absurdly high-pitched. 'I deserve it. I deserve it if they do . . . Not that I'm plaguey . . . Dizzy with standing, that's all. Better now.' He sat up.

'You stay away from us, Garvey.' Several of the players had drawn their knives.

Garvey's only response was to smile a misshapen smile powdered with grit off the stone floor.

'Are you feverish, Garvey?' said Lucie, his arm extended protectively across his daughter's body, as if to shield her from disease.

Garvey giggled. 'Not a bit of it.' He turned his face towards the altar end of the chapel, much as a bridegroom might turn his head towards his bride.

106

'He saved me, you see. He sent that Mason to carry all my sins and iniquity.'

The players passed their thoughts to each other in sidelong looks, all the circle round. But they flinched when Garvey rose clumsily to his knees. 'Didn't you see?' he piped. 'Didn't you see him take it from me and put it inside his own shirt? My sins—that's what was in that bag. He took them from me. He put them in here.' And Garvey mimed, with uncanny accuracy, how Colley the Mason had pushed the squire's purse of white velvet down inside his own shirt, under his armpit. 'I see it now. All this was for the saving of me. It was all to save me from the Fiery Pit. I blasphemed. But Colley paid the price. I'm well. I'm made clean! Look!' He stripped off his shirt and capered from outstretched dagger to outstretched dagger, displaying himself like the leper healed by Jesus showing himself to the High Priests. 'I'm clean! I'm clean! I'm saved! Look! No fever, no cough, no buboes! No Death! No Death! No Death!'

At the foot of the altar he stopped, his smooth, white plumpness daubed with bright colours by the sun through the stained glass. He stared down at his body, and large tears splashed on to the brilliant tattoos of light. He was filled with ecstasy at the miracle of his fat, sagging body.

Impulsively, Gabriel ran and hugged the playmaster. Shame drove him to it. A moment before he had been guilty of one damnable, wicked, fleeting moment of joy when he thought Garvey lay dead on the floor.

The company breathed out with one breath, and crossed themselves. All at once, they allowed themselves to believe that they would go on living.

Garvey had some difficulty in emerging from his ecstasy. He fingered Gabriel's hair. 'It's all right, boy. I know what I've done to you. I know what sins I've committed. But I'm going to make it all right. I'm going to Walsingham now. I'm going on pilgrimage to Walsingham, to ask your mother's forgiveness for my . . .'

'My mother?' As he said it, Gabriel's eye was caught by Lucie who put a finger up to his lips as if to say, 'Don't argue.'

'Yes, the Holy Virgin Mary, who showed herself to Englishmen at Walsingham. Wait a moment. I'm confused. Who is the mother of the angels? I'll find out! My head, it's going round now. It's full of words. But I'll get it straight at Walsingham. I'll walk all the way, and in my bare feet, too . . . You could pray for me, if you find the time, son. I know it's a lot to ask, but I'm not so black as I once was, you know. That Mason—he carried it off me, you see. And praying comes easy to the likes of you . . . I must be starting out now. It's a way to go, I think. And on foot.'

He took off his boots, and stood them tidily, side by side, the toes tucked under the altar cloth. His white feet slapped across the cold chapel floor, and he opened the barred door.

No importuning crowd spilled into the chapel; only the sunlight. Not a soul remained of the plaguey mob: not a dead body, not a live petitioner.

Where do the birds go when they die? They die in secret, and their bodies are never found in the open. All the village had gone to earth. Earth to earth. Only Colley remained.

They saw his body in the moat, where he had thrown himself to escape the mob.

The squire's white velvet purse had weighed him down, and though he had slipped it out of his jerkin and felt it sink past his feet, coins still seemed to be clinging to his armpit. He had felt them—round swelling lumps the size of gold coins. And feeling them, he had stopped swimming, thrown a wordless curse at the sky, then surrendered himself to the black cold beneath the surface of the moat. It swallowed him like a mouth.

They looked down from the bridge and saw the arms washed upwards, the plague swellings plainly visible. And they left him floating there—though Garvey swore to pray for his soul. 'As soon as I reach Walsingham!' he called over his shoulder. 'All this was for me, you know!' And he walked away from the manor as though he had arrived there as empty-handed, half-naked and alone as when he left.

CHAPTER TEN

THE PETITION

'BURN EVERYTHING,' said Lucie. 'It's the only way.'

So they put a torch to the Mason's wagon and, as the flames swept through the wooden base, a shower of warped and molten coins cascaded out on to the ground. A trickle of wax, a hiss of steaming ale, a molten wedge of congealed pots and pans, clots of silver, the black ash of canvas, a gout of feathers exploding into the air; and an eerie ringing of reforged wheelrims, wagon arches and barrel rings.

The pageant took longer to burn. The golden pavilion and the peacock feathers flared and were gone in an instant, but the Hill of Heaven took a long while to cave in, and Hell burned with a black, acrid smoke billowing out of its throat. The weather-vane glowed white hot on the ground, with ash tracing where its ribbons had been. And gold leaf fountained into the smoke, and fell so slowly, see-sawing through the heat-coggled air, that it appeared to be snowing gold. The mirrors over God's throne and Gabriel's shattered—bang! bang!—like two shots from a gun, and the pageant, which was lying on its back, sagged in on itself like a man breathing his last. The Garden of Eden burned down. The atlas of the Holy Land—Bethlehem, Jerusalem, Mount Horeb, Egypt and Jericho—all crumbled into the same heap of ash. The players tore off their costumes—demons and saints and girls—and pitched them into the flames. Lucie slipped the scarlet waistcoat off Gabriel's shoulders and skinned him of the white silk shirt. They burned in a tangle with the Devil's scaly serpent's skin and were indistinguishable. Gabriel said nothing, but his body leaned yearningly towards the fire.

Seeing how the wanton destruction of beautiful things galled and tormented the boy, Lucier said, 'You think that was beautiful? You should have seen the old pageants. There was one for every play of the cycle—one for *The Garden of Eden*, one for *The murder of Abel*, one for *The Sacrifice of Isaac*, one for *The destruction of the World* . . . That one was a phoenix. That could burn and still be there afterwards. Mountains fell and there were mountains again the next day. This? What's this? It never even saw Christ.'

As he spoke, he took out the whetted knife from his belt and, lifting Gabriel's curling hair, began to cut it off.

'Christ?' said Gabriel.

'Did you not notice? In all the time you've played with us, we've never played a Mystery with Christ in it.'

'Are there plays with Jesus in them?'

'Well of course there are, son. They're the flesh and core of the Mysteries. We only played the pith and peel, the pieces at either end . . .'

'You mean a man pretended to be Jesus?' said Gabriel incredulously.

'Why not? We pretended to be God and angels. Is it different?'

The knife sliced through the hair like a sickle harvesting corn, and the hair piled up around Gabriel's feet. Lucie dragged the knife blade up the back of Gabriel's neck: a terrible sensation of scraping stubble.

'Yes, it's different somehow. Who played Jesus?' he asked.

'I did, Gabriel. But Garvey liked my Lucifer better. It always got the crowds laughing.'

Izzie muttered, 'He didn't like the glory it brought you. He liked to shine out as God.'

'Speak ill of him now he's gone, do you?' said her father. 'Me, I don't choose to remember what's bad in a man . . . No, Gabriel, I've not played Christ now for upwards of two years.'

'But you still remember the lines?'

Lucie hesitated. 'Certainly I remember the lines.'

'So you'd best live for ever, hadn't you? . . . My mother said I should never cut my hair or I'd lose my strength, like Samson in the Bible.'

'And have you?'

Gabriel flexed his muscles, then set off to run. He ran from end to end of the yard and paused as he came back to the edge of the fire to peer down into a shattered mirror. Crazed like a pavement and as bald as a chicken, his head stared back at him.

'It will grow,' said Izzie.

'Who cares?' He shrugged, 'I'm not dead yet. That's what the playmaster told the squire. The Miracle-Worker's not dead yet . . . At least, *I'm* not.'

Under the Mason's wagon, the canvas wrapper burned away, lay his iron tools—chisel and mallet, goudge and spike. 'Are those clean now?' asked Gabriel crouching beside them.

'Yes. The fire's cleaned them, I reckon,' said Adam of Rochester.

'Can I have them, then?' The man shrugged and looked at him as if he were mad. He and the other members of the company were picking out shapeless ingots, precious gems and buckled coins, licking their fingers as they burnt them, as if they were pulling roast chestnuts out of a grate. Gabriel picked up the tools.

Shivering in their nakedness, and all shorn of their hair, the actors kept on only their stage boots as they

112

walked back the way they had come. The property wagon was still sprawled within sight of the monastery on its smashed undercarriage. It lay midway between the estate and the wedding village. There they shared garments. Those most coveted were the ones with pockets to hold all the valuables salvaged and brought away in fists. Rich men in gowns, dresses and Roman robes set off on foot to north, south, east and west. They would make a strange sight in the towns round about: clowns richer than knights or lords, who limped in wearing felt boots, to buy, buy and buy. The Mason's hired men were first to go, and their pockets bulged the most.

'Will we meet up in the spring, Lucie?' said Ydrys.

'As you like. But I don't reckon I'm fit for much.'

'Your heart?'

'Some such part of me. I won't be playing again, I know that.'

'What about the Words, though?' said Ydrys.

Lucie shrugged. 'Look where they got us. They've got no use for words back there where we've come from. They've finished with words. So have I.'

Izzie climbed down from the wagon, dressed in the man-sized gown of the Virgin Mary. It dangled past her fingertips, but she had bunched it up with a belt around her waist. She said, 'For friendship's sake come back and see us, Ydrys. We'll be at the deserted village. In the spring, you hear?'

'Yes, Izzie. Right.' And Ydrys walked off, looking several times over his shoulder at Lucie, who had 'finished with words'.

When everyone else had gone, Gabriel helped Lucie to mend the cart's wheel. The horse, having been abandoned in the traces for twenty-four hours, was utterly disgruntled. Feeling the wagon level again, it took off at a trot. They had to run after it, Izzie outstripping her father, but Gabriel, who was sensibly dressed in his old stoneworking hessian, outstripping her. He caught up, and reasoned with the horse.

He was soon embarrassed, therefore, to find himself back at the plague village, helping Lucie and Izzie to settle into one of the cottages, wondering why he had not left with the rest. It was when Izzie began to make him up a mattress to sleep on that he said, 'Well, just tonight. Then I'd best be going.'

'Oh?'

'And can I have twenty shillings, please?' he said, shuffling his feet.

'You can have twenty pounds, Gabriel. You're not poor,' said Lucie.

'Well, I'd best find a master-mason. I've got Colley's tools. Maybe I can find someone to apprentice me. If I have the money.'

Lucie counted out twenty gold pieces—the ones least defaced by heat—on to the table. 'There you are, then. You should be able to buy your way into any Mystery you choose with that. I had hoped you'd stay on. Through the winter. With us.'

'You don't want me.'

'Not for miracle-working, no.'

'I mean, if the pageant's finished, you don't need me to learn the Words.'

'No, no,' said Lucie with an airy, dismissive wave of his hand. 'Our pageant's done for. Some plays may live on—in York or Wakefield or the like. They write down their verses there . . .'

'And besides, Izzie knows them all,' Gabriel blurted out. 'So you don't need me.'

Embarrassed, Izzie busied herself with the bed-making, putting up her hand repeatedly to keep in place the headscarf over her shaved head. Out of the corner of her eye she looked, though, to see if her father was angry at the idea of a mere woman knowing the Words.

Lucie whistled sharply to catch her attention, then beckoned her over to stand beside him. He caught hold of her hand as it went up once more to her headscarf, and he held it tight against his side. 'I know she does, Gabriel. I know she knows them. And one day she'll maybe marry and have sons, and pass the Words on to them. But only if she chooses. The Words aren't worth one fraction of a second of sadness for a daughter of mine:

"For who would babes and bairns distress
    Should into salty sea no less
  Be thrown with millstone round his neck
    To be like any ship y-wrecked."'

'Who said that?' asked Gabriel, and Izzie laughed and clapped her hands. Lucie looked slightly appalled by his ignorance.

'Christ Jesus said it, Gabriel. Leastways his verses in the Mystery . . .'

'Ah well, you see I never heard those ones,' said Gabriel quickly. 'If I stayed on, you could maybe teach . . . tell me them.'

Lucie looked dubious and uneasy. 'Maybe. Not for playing, mind! The pageant's dead and gone.'

'So, in the name of God *why do you want me?*' demanded Gabriel in exasperation.

Lucie seemed at a loss for words. He looked at Izzie, but she was wearing her arms folded and a look of smug curiosity, waiting to hear what he would say. So Lucie shrugged and threw up his hands in the way that suddenly betrayed his French stock:

'Well, because we *like* you, of course!'

A month later, they began stripping down the provision cart to use for a pageant. There were other carts scattered, in various stages of decay, around the hastily abandoned village: no shortage of wood, no shortage of time, as the tracks in and out of the place filled up with mud. They had all winter.

115

One day the family returned who had once lived in the cottage occupied now by Lucie, Izzie and Gabriel. They had found no permanent livelihood or shelter away from their disease-ridden village. They, too, reasoned that Death, having gorged itself on their neighbours, would have long since moved on. When they found their home occupied by a man and two children, they simply stood in the doorway with faces as empty as begging bowls, and made no complaint. They had long since stopped expecting the world to deal kindly with them: they had used up their good fortune by remaining alive when the Plague came.

'We'll go at once!' said Izzie, jumping up. There were garments half-made and for mending bunched beneath her belt again, though she wore dresses now.

But the family simply shrugged and patted the air and went to the far end of the street, and moved into a cottage whose roof did not leak. They did not come near Lucie, Izzie or Gabriel, and had to be kept from starving with little presents of food left furtively on their threshold. It was rather like leaving tributes at an altar.

While Gabriel was emptying the cart of all remaining rubbish, ready for painting, he found some of the parchment petitions. When squirreling away the wax seals, Colley had thrown the parchments into the property wagon as so much litter. Gabriel put them all into a canvas bag and hung them on a nail inside the cottage door.

The pageant they built was crude—a ladder and a low plinth for God to sit on, a single trapdoor straight out on to the grass, a curtain across to conceal anyone who used it. Lucie's attitude to it was a mixture of contempt and childlike delight. He swore he would never use it, but he wished it were better. He said he hadn't the strength to act on it, and yet he exhausted himself in making it roadworthy. When there was snow lying on it, he fervently hoped the whole thing

116

would melt away in the thaw. And when the snow thawed and took with it the paint they had daubed it with, he was out there picking off the remaining flakes of paint, and cursing with disappointment. He turned round to find the man from the other end of the village standing behind him, dubiously shaking his head.

'What that needs is a coat of paint,' he said dolefully. His name was Alan Reddler, and painting and dyeing were his trade.

The first play they mounted was for Alan and his family—to celebrate the completion of the pageant. A sketchy version of *Noah and the Flood*, it was, with Lucie as God, and Gabriel and Izzie playing Mr and Mrs Noah. It seemed appropriate. The village felt rather as if it were a hopeful ark floating in isolation while the rest of the world was covered over, hidden from sight by watery winter.

The family watched it with their solemn, empty faces, standing at a great distance from the stage. Alan said, 'I remember seeing the life of Christ Jesus acted out one time. You don't know it, I suppose?'

'I don't?' said Lucie.

'You do?' Alan quickly suppressed the glimmer of excitement in his eye, but he could not conceal the quickening of his step as he walked back to his end of the village. Next day he came along carrying a huge, man-sized wooden cross, and propped it up against the pageant. 'You'll maybe be needing one if you remember the Jesus play,' he said flatly, out of his blank face, keeping his distance all the while.

On the first day of spring, the weather-vane fell off the church. Gabriel thought it was a sign. He ran with it, stumbling under the weight, to show Lucie.

Lucie was squatting on his bed-roll, sweating profusely, with one hand spread on his chest as

117

though making a vow. The shadows of his face were green. 'What do you want?' he snapped, as Gabriel kicked open the door for want of a free hand. 'Stealing from the church now, are you?'

Gabriel set down the rusty metal bird, dismissing the thing with a jab of his foot. 'I was just going to put it back,' he lied. 'I wanted to ask you something.'

'Not now, boy, please.'

Gabriel ignored Lucie's obvious desire to be left alone, and took down the canvas bag from the nail behind the door. 'Is it right that monks can read? All of them?'

'Gabriel. Not now . . .'

'It's important. I've been thinking about these requests for miracles. We ought to have somebody pray for the people who wrote them.'

Lucie lay back on his bed and stared up at the cobwebbed planks under the thatch. 'Are they on your conscience, lad?'

'That's it. They're on my conscience. What say I take them over to that monastery on the moor—with some money—and ask the monks to say some masses?'

'And bring the law down on our heads? You're mad boy. You'd have us excommunicated and hanged inside a month. It's confessing to our fraud.' The blue blood vessels were entwining Lucie's throat again and strangling his speech.

'We could say we found them,' said Gabriel wheedlingly.

'Monks aren't stupid, boy. It's in the nature of monks not to be stupid.'

'To look at me, no one would take me for the Miracle-Worker,' Gabriel persisted, and he grinned and rubbed his short head of hair which had barely grown long enough for a single curl.

His smile met with no response. Lucie's thoughts were entirely given over to the pain in his chest; he was overrun with pain. 'Send Izzie to me, will you?' he said.

'All right,' said Gabriel blithely, as if he had noticed nothing wrong. 'Then I'll go to the monastery, I think. It's on my conscience, you see.' He ran and kissed Lucie on the forehead, as if it was something he did routinely every day. Then he darted out of the room, pausing only when he reached the barn, to lean against the door and breathe deeply. 'Izzie! Your father wants you!' he called to her, as he rode the wagon pony up on to the crisp, brittle moor where every blade of grass and bushy twig was petrified by frost.

He was beginning to panic, thinking that he had strayed off the route, when the monastery at last came into sight. Then he seemed to recognize every feature of the place, right down to the boulder which had sheared the wheel off the property wagon, on that horrible night. He rode straight up to the gateway of the monastery, not daring to stop for second thoughts, and said to the first monk he saw, 'Can you read and write?'

The monk, wearing a black tabard over a white habit, only stared at him, but halted beside a low doorway and tossed his head in a summons. Gabriel tied up his pony and followed him. Inside the doorway, a spiral stone staircase climbed, within the thickness of the massive walls. A draught chased up the steps like a dog snapping at their heels, and the sound of the door slamming behind them spiralled on ahead. It was bitterly cold, and light trickled in on only every second twist in the stairs. Gabriel's resolve drained away with every step. Just when his eyes were adjusting to the gloom, the novice ahead of him threw open a door, and Gabriel emerged into pale but blinding sunlight flaring in low through the window of the gallery.

Sitting in the path of the light, which cascaded over

119

his head and shoulders and his white robe, sat a man of perhaps thirty years. His curly red hair circled his shining tonsure like a wreath of flowers and, as he stood up, the sun seemed to shine clean through his woollen habit without silhouetting a body inside it. To Gabriel he looked just like . . .

'What's the matter, little brother. Don't be shy,' said the Cistercian. 'I'm the Prior. Can I help you at all? Have you sickness at home? Is it your mother who's sent you? It's not hunger that brought you, I know. I've seen thinner lambs at Eastertide. Come forward. Speak to me. Our cells may be cold as a dip in the sea, but our hearts are still warm, thank God.'

'Thank God,' mumbled Gabriel, scuffing forwards. He felt horribly aware, all of a sudden, of a winter's-worth of grime on him. 'I have some money . . . and a favour to ask . . .'

Standing waiting in the yard, while another pony was being saddled, Gabriel asked to see the monastery chapel. It was pointed out to him—a small, plain, vaulted room with only a table for an altar and gaily-painted saints carved in wood standing about like skittles at a fair. There was a bunch of winter aconites on the table, and stripes of sunshine on the floor alternated with deep darkness. There was no church treasure chest as Gabriel had hoped. But at least there were no monks in there praying either.

Even a boy who was used to climbing trees might have thought twice about climbing the walls of an undecorated chapel. But Gabriel had spent a year as a stonemason's apprentice, clinging to the rafters and cornices of holy buildings, finishing off or preparing the stone. He was out of practice, but he found no difficulty in scaling the window carvings and balancing on the icy stone arch while he pushed the canvas bag and all its petitions into a stone loop in the lowest vaulting. He jumped down, and was sitting on the floor of the nave putting on his boots again when the Friar's appointed monk tracked him down.

'Is it you I'm to accompany, little brother?' said the monk, somewhat taken aback.

'It is. We've plenty of room for you. And food. But if you could bring a bed-roll . . .'

The monk looked Gabriel over warily and said, 'God will provide, I daresay. And you can tell me my duties as we go.'

As they rode out of the low narrow gate, their knees banging, their heads ducked, the other monks were mustering for the Holy Office of Vespers. Their chanting rose up through the vaulted roof of the Cistercian chapel.

When they got back, Lucier was sitting in a chair outside the door of the house, watching Alan and his sons batten the church weather-vane to the corner of the little pageant. He seemed greatly recovered, and resigned to the idea of using what the church so obligingly had offered. But he was dismayed, in the circumstances, to see Gabriel ride off the moor and up the street in the company of a young monk. Alan snatched up an osier basket and hung it on the cockerel's rusty head to hide it.

The more he thought about it, the worse Lucie liked the idea of Gabriel being accompanied by a monk. Would the Archbishop's Summoner be following close behind with warrants for their arrest? Lucier stood up, with his hand spread across his breastbone as if to protect his heart from the jolt, and weighed up the possibilities of escape. Izzie watched the ponies' approach from the cart top, through narrowed, scowling eyes.

'Lucie, this is Brother Michael,' said Gabriel, slithering off his pony. He had meant to be casual, off-hand, collected and rather grand. As it was, he stood in front of Lucie's chair leaping from foot to foot and gesticulating wildly. 'I've borrowed him! He can read and write! He's got pens and paper, too! I offered the Prior my twenty pounds but he wouldn't take it. All he wants is a fair copy to keep in his library!'

'Gabriel, what is this? What are you telling me? What have you done with the petitions?'

'Nothing. Shshsh,' said Gabriel, blushing. 'That was something else. I'll tell you after. In private. Don't you understand? I've brought you a writer! You tell the verses to Brother Michael, and he writes them down! See? Every single word! Nothing lost! You don't have to worry any more. He's foreign, too. The Prior is foreign. His father comes from Italy. And so clever! He speaks Italian and English and Latin.' Gabriel pulled the saddle-bags off the monk's pony and struggled inside the house with them.

'Quite a man, this prior,' said Lucie, looking penetratingly into the young monk's face.

'He has put me at your service, sir,' replied the monk, 'for the love this boy bears you. Is this the pageant? My father used to play Judas in the Cordwainer's Mystery every Corpus Christi Day.'

A sudden thaw set in in Lucier, and the rigid muscles of his face softened. His black eyes flickered, and he drew the monk over by his sleeve to look at the pageant more closely. 'Is that a fact? Where was that? Locally? Did you have the words put down?'

'Of course. For the Bishop to censor. Though we learned them by word of mouth, of course. My father wasn't a reading man.'

'Learned them? You mean you knew some yourself?'

'Oh Judas I knew, naturally. Didn't we hear father talking it day and night round the house in the days before Corpus Christi? Of course it's left me now. All forgotten.'

122

'Never! A man doesn't forget what he's known! Of course, it won't be the same verses I know . . . I'm a Dover man, myself—out of France—but we could blend the two, your Judas and mine!'

Izzie left them deep in animated conversation—the monk laughing out loud as he realized he was being lured into an acting profession—and went inside the house to find Gabriel.

He had set out the costly paper, ink and pens with geometric precision on the table and was setting a stool for the scribe to sit on. His jubilant excitement had melted away.

'That was a gentle thing you did there,' she said.

'Did I do right, Izzie? I'd much rather he went on acting and I went on learning. But I'm so slow! And he won't be fit to act when the spring comes, I'm sure of it. Will he?'

'No. He won't be fit.'

'And at least the Words will be there. For *someone* to read.'

'Yes, at least the Words will be there.'

Gabriel suddenly slapped the fist of his hand down on the pile of paper and crumpled the topmost sheet. 'But *we* won't be able to read it, and anyway . . . I don't want Lucie to die,' he hissed ferociously. 'And he will, won't he?'

So she went and gave him a hug. 'And why shouldn't he? With nothing left to fret about? He deserves a good rest. And think of the pageants there'll be in Heaven.' And she smoothed out the crumpled paper and neatened the desk still more, and found a wad of rag to stop the stool wobbling. Then she insisted, 'It was a very kind thing you did . . . even if you did risk us all getting hung!'

In the first week of good weather, over half the acting members of the Miracle Pageant came back to the plague village, just to see how their old friend Lucier was faring. They had all been working at stone-gathering, keeping their pageant money out of sight for fear the constables mark them as robbers or miracle-workers. Adam of Rochester, Jack of Longleigh, and Ydrys were first to arrive. They stopped and wondered at the crude little pageant parked outside the cottage, stroking its paintwork and prying into the winches and traps. They started exchanging recollections of older pageants in their own home towns. There was some unspoken understanding, however, that the miracle business was not to be mentioned. And they forgot to knock at the door and make themselves known to the people inside.

When Izzie came out, hearing voices, she found them drawing tally marks in the dust, counting up the number of different roles they could play between them. She signalled that they should lower their voices and follow her round the building to a new window smashed through the wall of the cottage. It let in sunlight from late morning till late evening, casting it across the square of a table in the middle of the room.

Jack of Longleigh, Adam of Rochester, and Ydrys obediently fell silent, thinking that perhaps they had arrived in time to witness the last ebbing breaths of their one-time Lucifer. They queued, docile and long-faced, by the window, their caps in their hands, waiting to be allowed to peep inside.

On the bed there indeed lay a man. But it was not a man they had ever seen before. He seemed to be dozing out of sheer idleness, with his head against the wall. A woman with two young boys round her skirts was preparing a meal, perched on a stool with a pottery bowl on her knees. At the table sat a young Cistercian monk, and at either elbow sat Lucier and Gabriel watching him copy one page of writing from another. Their forefingers imitated the movements of the pen, looping and daubing across the table-top, while their lips mouthed silently the same slow words.

'The three wise monkeys,' Izzie whispered, giggling. 'See no evil. Hear no evil. Speak no evil. Do you see how well my father looks? The Cistercians are all herbalists, and Alan's wife cooks so much better than me.'

'I didn't recognize him!'

'Nor me.'

Just then, the monk found difficulty in seeing the page he was copying. Four round shadows had blocked out all the light from the window. He looked up, frowning, and started almost out of his skin as he saw four heads gawping in. Then Gabriel jumped up and rushed outdoors to greet them. And Lucier followed with that same loping, economical, elegant stride, and now as grey-haired, too, as a wolf.

Alan the Reddler was woken up by all the greetings:

'Still a widow, are you, Izzie?'
'Got your curls back then, boy . . .'
'This is Michael: he knows Judas!'

'. . . you old lizard, Lucie! What's the Devil been eating to get such flesh on him?'

The monk sealed his flask of ink and wrapped his pens, and the woman wiped her hands and removed the Mystery scripts to a high shelf where they could come to no harm. 'Best fetch more furniture, Alan,' she said to her bleary husband. 'Looks like we'll be eleven sitting down to dinner.'

CHAPTER ELEVEN

THE LAST PERFORMANCE

'THINK OF the pageants in Heaven!'

Gabriel watched the stately clouds move across the sky: an entire cycle of pageant wagons, with streamers and gantries and lofty white walls. There were so many, moving so fast, that they made him dizzy. As far as he could see, not one angel perched on their peaks.

He was crouching underneath the pageant, looking up at the sky through the central trapdoor, waiting to be created out of a rib in Adam's chest and become First Woman. He had on the long white cloak which signified to the audience that he was wearing nothing at all. But he could not quite help wondering if anyone would mistake him, Gabriel, for a naked lady. He tried to think back to the first Mystery he had seen, but he could only remember 'Eve' as that unshaven, white-skinned man who had left them outside the lock-up in Greathaven and gone to find work on the boats. Gabriel wrapped the white cloak tighter around him, and pulled his curly hair as far down to his shoulders as he could. He could see Lucier waiting behind the pageant in his serpent's costume for his cue to emerge from the Mouth of Hell and tempt Eve with the forbidden fruit. 'Such a nice face,' thought Gabriel. 'He really shouldn't play Lucifer.'

Rolande and Ydrys sat cross-legged on the ground nearby, playing their music. The events of the year seemed to have washed over them and left them unaltered. Their role had never changed. Their music would always be needed—long after the Mystery Plays disappeared.

Garvey was gone, but up above a new God was creating the World all over again in verse: the whales, the trees, the Garden of Eden, Adam ... and Eve. Gabriel climbed up the ladder, appearing to rise out of the rib-cage of First Man, who was lying across the front lip of the trapdoor. A pretty little boy not above six boggled at Gabriel from the front row and cried out, 'Ma! Look at the lady! God made a lady, did you see?' At the appearance of the Devil, the child hid his face in his mother's lap. (So Lucie could not have changed so much.)

After the greyness and isolation of winter, the crowds seemed a mad profusion of seething colour, all the time moving, all the time talking. And so many eyes! Gabriel fixed his gaze on the cloud pageants overhead or on Adam or on Lucifer or on God, rather than be distracted by the restless crowd. Besides—there was no time these days for playing the Wishing Game, not with so many lines to remember.

Alan the Reddler made an uneasy angel, driving Adam and Eve out of the Garden of Eden. He would leave them soon—as soon as he found a place that pleased him and set up home, or found work at his own mystery of painting, dyeing and carpentry. Gabriel would miss the wife's cooking and the little children, who made him feel almost a grown man.

Everything went on changing. Nothing ever remained the same. Even now that times were good, Gabriel could not say, 'Stop! That's fine. No more alterations needed.' Everything went on changing. What next?

Lucifer pointed out to Eve the forbidden apple on the flat tree painted on to the back panel of the cart. The apple sat on a small ledge jutting out from the

127

wall. Gabriel reached up to take it, but hesitated. What if he did not take it? If he did not, then perhaps the whole action could stop—freeze—with him and his friends all captive together in this little Garden of Eden where there was no evil and only endless, unchanging cheerfulness.

> 'Nor will I be to God foreswore.
> There let it hang for evermore,
> That sweet, forbidden fruit.'

He grinned wickedly at Lucie as if to say, 'There now. What are you going to do now, playmaster? Shall we change the course of history, you and I?'

Lucie raised his eyebrows and made great, exaggerated play of his astonishment, while he thought up a fitting reply. It was not the first time they had played this mischievous game with each other, on stage.

> 'Eve! Take the fruit and eat it all.
> Man's fixed fate it is to fall.
> What story else could we devise
> Who live by playing Mysteries?'

The audience gave a great cheer, recognizing that the actors were making fun of them and of each other. Gabriel reached up and took the apple and bit into it greedily. He woke First Man and made him eat, too, and 'Adam' threw the apple core out over the crowd's heads.

It arced through the air, drawing every eye after it, so that, as the crowd gaped upwards, Gabriel and Adam could turn inside out their white cloaks and show the red lining, to signify their change from innocents to guilty sinners. As Gabriel reversed his cape and retied the cord at his throat, his eye too was following the apple core as it fell into the crowd and shattered against a yeoman's shoulder.

First Man looked down and saw that he was naked,

and hurried away to find fig leaves to cover himself . . .
But when he looked over his shoulder, expecting Eve
to be doing much the same, she was heading in quite a
different direction.

To the crowd's consternation, Eve, dropping her
red cloak, had hurled herself off the front of the cart
and was pushing through the crowd, quite plainly a
boy in breeches, shirt and felt boots. He clambered
over a bench, vaulted over a nestle of children on the
ground, and failed to dodge a pie-seller. Picking
himself up, he threw his arms around the yeoman who
was still plucking shreds of apple off his jerkin.

'Father, it's me! Gabriel! It's me! I can write! The
Mason's dead. I've still got my twenty shillings. And I
can read—not Latin, of course! It's me, Father! You
do know me, don't you?'

'I was thinking the lady looked a mite like my boy,'
said the yeoman, slowly, unperturbably, like a dray-
horse picking its way through a bog. 'But I didn't like
to disturb the Mystery. There, there. What did they
want to go shying apples at your old father for, eh?
There, there. Your mother's in for a bit of a surprise, I
daresay? That hair of yours is getting right long.
Don't you have no shears, lad? There's some manner
of explaining all this, I daresay. There, there. Am I to
be mobbed by all these folk for want of an end to their
Mystery? Yep, seems like I am.' And he picked up
Gabriel with just one arm round his hips, and
stumped stolidly away with him to the privacy of the
inn.

On the edge of the stage, the snake-like Devil,
Lucifer, stood watching the father carry his son away
like a stook of yellow corn in his arms, up the village
street. Down at Lucifer's feet, in front of the stage, a
girl with long, black hair stood on tip-toe but still
could not see over the heads of the crowd. After a
moment, Lucifer reached down one hand and lifted
the girl up on to the stage. He picked up the red and

white cloak and wrapped it around her shoulders, red side outwards. The crowd murmured uneasily. A girl in a pageant? It was unthinkable.

Lucifer turned on them with such ferocity that some actually fell backwards off their benches. 'Well? You want a Mystery, don't you? Jesu, if it was good enough for God, what have *you* got to carp about? He built Himself a pageant, didn't He? The pageant to end all pageants. Too wide to fit across a pack-bridge, I can tell you! As wide as from there to there!' (He pointed to opposite horizons.) 'Just as many girls as boys! Girls and boys and angels and fathers and sons and daughters. And devils! Oh yes, plenty of devils! Whole packs of devils!' He was pointing out into the audience as he said it. 'And then there are players— but they don't signify, of course!' And he exited so violently down the throat of Hell that he ripped the tongue and set the snout bobbing as if Hell were about to sneeze.

Abashed, the audience sat with their hands on their knees, and watched on solemnly: a strange Mystery, with no laughter. At the end, Rolande and Ydrys had to play two verses of music before the crowd could be persuaded to get up and dance.

Izzie joined in the circle-dance, and wanted her father to join in too. People did not want to hold hands with either of them at first, but without her red cloak to remind them of sin, they quickly forgot who Izzie was. They would not on any account join hands with Lucifer.

Lucier was accustomed to it: the wry grins as they acknowledged he was only a man in costume; the superstitious snatching away of their hands for fear he was a little bit more. Normally it amused him. Today he felt as slighted as a leper.

Izzie held hands with him. 'He'll come back, you know. Gabriel will come back,' she said as they danced.

'Never. He's got what he wants. We're melted out of his memory, you take my word.' Lucier danced aggressively, mechanically, joylessly.

Izzie repeated, as if she had not heard him, 'He'll be back, you'll see. Just as soon as he's made his greetings and told his news.'

'And what for, can I ask? He's got one father, hasn't he?' Lucifer's face was so devil-like as he said it that he frightened even Izzie, a thing he had never done on stage. 'I don't want him back. I don't want the honour of knowing his father, thank you Miss. "Here, father, this is my . . ." What would he say? ". . . this is my teacher! This is my playmaster! This is . . ."' The circle broke while the dancers whirled each other in pairs. As they spun round, Lucier's grip was hurting his daughter's hands. But gradually she drew him round and out, round and out of the mêlée. And there stood Gabriel and his father.

'You'll be supping with us, then?' said the yeoman. 'Gabriel's told us of yourself and your daughter.'

Lucier did not speak.

'Are you angry with me, Lucie? For spoiling the Mystery?' said Gabriel anxiously.

Lucier shrugged. 'I don't think we have time, sir. We move on, you know. All the time. We'll probably be in Exeter by tomorrow night.'

'Lucie!' cried Gabriel. 'Not a day? Not a single night at home?'

Lucier refocused his eyes on Gabriel and frowned. 'What?'

'That's a rum name to be calling the man,' said Gabriel's father. 'Doesn't the playmaster have a proper name, Gabriel?'

Miserably, Gabriel collected himself. 'Oh. Oh yes. Lucie, this is my father, yeoman Gabriel of the Banks. And Father, these are my friends, Jean and Izzie Lucier of Dover out of France . . . Not one night, Lucie? Not one?'

'*Friends*,' said Lucie to nobody but himself. 'I hadn't thought of that one.'

'And you won't even let the boy stay long enough to see his mother?' said the yeoman without animosity. 'I know he's got a living to earn, but surely a day can't hurt.'

Lucier stared. 'Gabriel, what have you been telling your father? You're not bound to the Mysteries. You're home now. You've finished with us. You've done with travelling about.'

Gabriel's face dropped even further. 'But I'm a Mystery Player! That's my trade! I'm Eve! Aren't I? You can't do without me ... Can you?' he said pleadingly. He did not understand the shout of laughter the Frenchman gave.

'That's a fact, boy, we can't.' He did not look into Gabriel's face but into the yeoman's. 'But how can a father do without his boy?'

The father put both hands on his son's shoulders and pushed him a step or two towards Lucier. 'The lad's got to make a living. He's got to have a trade. That's how life is, though it takes a boy away from his home. As long as he's in good hands, his mother won't fret. And I can tell from a half-hour's converse with him that he's in good hands. I'll tell you something, Frenchman. It's a fortunate man with more than one son—and I'm such. And it's a more fortunate boy yet with more than one father—and Gabriel's such.'

He would have shaken hands with Lucier, but the playmaster turned abruptly on his heel and disappeared behind the pageant.

'Where's he gone?' said Gabriel.

'He'll be back,' said Izzie. 'Believe me, I do know when people are coming back ... Oh, and we will be staying over, Yeoman Gabriel, sir. At least a week. My father doesn't always mean what he says.'

After another unaccountable minute, Lucier emerged from behind the pageant wiping his eyes on a piece of his costume.

'Fool Frenchmen,' said the yeoman with a snort of laughter.

But Izzie, watching the figure loping towards them with his strange, wolf-like walk, suddenly knew how the Devil will look on the day of his Redemption.